x18

~~H. C. Kneil~~

William F. Kneil

A/14/14

# England is My Village

*by the same author*

*

THE FLYING SHADOW
THE WORLD OWES ME A LIVING

# ENGLAND IS MY VILLAGE

by
JOHN LLEWELYN RHYS
(Flight Lieutenant J. Ll. Rees, R.A.F.)

*with a Preface by*
JANE OLIVER

FABER AND FABER LIMITED
24 Russell Square
London

*First Published in January Mcmxli*
*by Faber and Faber Limited*
24 *Russell Square, London, W.C.*1
*Second Impression February Mcmxli*
*Third Impression May Mcmxli*
*Fourth Impression September Mcmxli*
*Printed in Great Britain by*
*Western Printing Services Limited, Bristol*

FOR MY WIFE

In his loneliness and fixedness he yearneth towards the journeying Moon, and the stars that still sojourn, yet still move onward; and everywhere the blue sky belongs to them, and is their appointed rest and their native country and their own natural homes, which they enter unannounced, as lords that are certainly expected, and yet there is a silent joy at their arrival.

SAMUEL TAYLOR COLERIDGE,
*The Rime of the Ancient Mariner.*

# Preface

It is not often that the pattern of a life emerges as clearly as that of John Llewelyn Rhys. So often age or ineptitude overlay promise and greatness is mocked by the wrong kind of success. This was not true of him. The shape of his life is as clear and purposeful as the strenuous arc of a drawn bow just before the arrow leaves it.

He wanted to fly and he wanted to write. He did both. His loyalties were simple: his family, his friends and his job. I do not know when the desire to fly first took him; perhaps, as he suggests in one of his own stories, in the days of the last war, when young men from the Royal Flying Corps came to his father's Rectory in Wales and awed a small boy with their wings. But the determination to be a writer goes further back, for his father, the present Vicar of Arthog, still possesses the short story which the author dictated to him because he had not yet learned to make his letters.

The usual process of public-school education did nothing to shake his determination, which was strong enough to make him unwilling to take the chance of going to Oxford because he knew that his true bent was elsewhere. For, though other jobs came first, his two ambitions had already twisted together, never to be separated again. He was to live by flying, and it was of flying that he wrote.

It was not till 1934 that he took his A licence at Cardiff. In 1935 he became a Sergeant Pilot in the Royal Air Force Reserve, and already the first story of this collection, "Test Flight", had appeared. During the winter of that year, on sick leave, he wrote his first novel, *The Flying Shadow*, from which the lovely little fragment, "Remembered on Waking", comes. The book was published in September 1936, just as another author, of whom he had probably never heard, was taking her A licence at Carlisle. And that author, who had also been caught by the air, did something she had never done before and will never do again; she wrote to John Rhys in astonished appreciation of a book which caught so exactly the terror and loveliness of flight.

I have his answer still, the first of many letters, the beginning of a friendship which was to belong to both his worlds, to be full of argument and the delight of equal enthusiasm. We talked interminably, almost always about writing and flying: on Hampstead Heath, in little country pubs, on the cat-haunted lawn of a house in St. John's Wood, in the Regency cottage by the Canal past which the barges churned, horse-towed or donkey-engined, hooting eerily for the bridge. There he would explain the intricacies of a flick half-roll and a rocket loop, while I corrected the spelling which was only slightly worse than my own.

He was flying continually now, for in 1936 he was gazetted as an Acting Pilot Officer in the Royal Air Force itself. His second novel, *The World Owes Me a Living*, from which the story called "Record Flight" is taken, was being written during 1937, and discussed on every short leave, whenever he got a chance to flog his little car up to London with a bundle of papers and an enormous box of chocolates in the back.

He was writing short stories too, of which "Too Young to Live", "Return to Life", and "Night

Exercise" belong to the precarious last years of peace, each showing a different aspect of an airman's life. He was teaching himself both his art and his craft. Writing never came easy to him. He had none of the slickness of the superficial author. He wrote, on the contrary, with increasing difficulty and stress as he gained experience. It was as if he were intent on compelling words to obey him, at whatever cost, through whatever fury of writing and re-writing, and all the scored and discarded sheets through which his pencil ripped. His goal was a simplicity which expressed with utter fidelity only and all his thought. He cut continually, paring away every inessential, his work gathering momentum with each ferocious stroke, but never satisfying him, who only reached one stage of achievement to look beyond it to the next.

It is difficult to assess the effect produced by constant, exacting and routine flight (as opposed to occasional light-hearted trips in hired Moths) on a man's make-up. Undoubtedly it does something, even to the toughest. One has only to see how in every gathering the flying men gravitate together, to talk the most engrossing shop in the world, to know that their calling takes them, with a certain arrogance, perhaps, but with great simplicity, apart.

The effect of flight on a creative artist is of necessity far greater. It imposes on a highly-geared nervous system certain stresses of which we know nothing. Fear, fatigue and exaltation combine, perhaps, to produce a friction sufficient to burn away the clutter of inessential things which cumber most of our lives and strip the main fabric bare. I think that it did something of the sort to John, heightening his perceptions, his capacity for suffering and joy, giving him a delight in absurdity and riot, in such contrasting things as the roaring company of his friends in smoke-hazed bars, the jigging figures of a film cartoon, the quiet safety of nights in his own home which held off the loneliness known by the men who fly constantly through darkness and in danger, a loneliness at which we others who wait for their return can only guess.

That loneliness went with him always. So he could write in *The Flying Shadow*: "sometimes when I can't sleep and it's cold and black and I feel afraid to die, I think to myself: 'Soon she'll be by my side, I shall put out my hand and touch her, and there'll be an end of loneliness.' "

And yet in other moods: "So it is that even in love we live apart, shut into our own lives . . . we shall be as two pilots flying wing-tip to wing-tip, who, for all their nearness and understanding, each of the other, can only communicate by clumsy and laborious effort."

The discipline of his work in the air, the terseness of phrase produced in a man who must handle the complex mechanism of enormous machines as a matter of course, gave to his writing something of its austerity and its mysticism. He wrote that "a sense of terrible power, the earth rolling and dropping out of sight, the calm confidence born in the conquest of fear and in the consciousness of absolute mastery that had been developed in the matrix of experience, would flood his mind with a strange peace. And in that peace he would find the stillness of spirit that is akin to the stillness of the body when the mind is netted by sleep. . . ."

Flying played too large a part in his consciousness for him to write merely of life in flying terms. He wrote, rather, of flying in terms of life. Towards death he had not only the average pilot's fatalistic attitude, but something more, a profound curiosity, an occasionally expressed, often contradicted instinct that it represented, not the extinction, but the achievement of life itself. So he could write of a first solo as "a triumph of individuality, like death . . .". Of a first parachute drop: "The fear was so awful that it amounted to an ecstasy. I felt something familiar about it, as if I'd been through it all before, as if I'd known it was going to happen all my life. . . . I remember wondering if it felt like that to die—I mean the fear and the sense of familiarity and then the great calm. . . ."

The momentum of his personal life was changing now. He wanted more, risked more, looked further. We had worked together since 1936. On Lady Day, 1939, we were married. *The World Owes Me a Living* was published in April, and in May his promotion to Flying Officer came through.

Recognition was coming quickly. But so was the war. His new book was serialized by the *News Chronicle*, the film rights were sold, another book begun. It was never finished, for only one chapter had been written by September. Short stories such as "You've Got to be Dumb to be Happy" were completed under war conditions. 'The Man who was Dead' followed early in 1940. But he was writing less, inevitably, as the war went on. His work in the Royal Air Force was too exacting. Only occasionally, during the short, thunder-sun-lit hours of leave, an idea would force itself upon him too strongly to be ignored. Such was his last story, "England is My Village", published in the United States by *Colliers* in June, and by the *Sunday Chronicle* in July. He was a Flight Lieutenant now, with responsibilities heavier than any which had gone before. But, like all the others, he made little of them so that I might be less afraid.

We spent the last week-end of July on leave in the New Forest. We had never been happier, talking of the chances of a few days' leave in Cornwall at the end of August, discussing the book of short stories which had been in his mind all summer. He went back to duty on the evening of Sunday, the 4th of August. Next day he was killed on active service.

And so it has fallen to me to complete the arrangements for this book, to carry out exactly the wishes he had already expressed. This I have tried to do. What he would have achieved, had things been otherwise, one can only guess. It is not for me to attempt to estimate his work. As he would always say: "You're prejudiced. You're my wife." It is only my personal belief that he might, one day, have come to speak for his generation. Instead—— And yet, looking back on his work and the years we had together which were bound up with it, I cannot feel despair that we had so little, but only amazement that we had so much.

JANE OLIVER

*5th September* 1940

# Contents

# England is My Village

# England is My Village

When the old man came into the ante-room the young officers began to rise in their chairs but he waved them back with an impatient gesture. It was warm and comfortable in there and the tenor of idle chatter continued: one could hear the crackle of a newspaper page and the sound of bidding from the four who were playing a Chinese game in the corner, their minds apparently intent on the little walls of white blocks on the table before them.

Beneath the Wing Commander's arm were a number of files. On the outside of the files was a map. Robert recognized its shape and his heart kicked inside him. And now every pilot in the Squadron was watching the Senior Officer, watching him without movement of head, watching him while seeming to read, watching him while crying "Three Characters". The Old Man nodded, first at one, then another, and finally at Robert. Silently they rose to their feet, leaving their circle of friends, their reading, their Chinese game, and filed into the neighbouring room. When they had gone the lazy murmur of conversation continued, watchers filled the places at the game, another officer picked up the copy of *The Field* that Robert had been reading.

. . . . .

The Wing Commander stood by the grand piano waiting for them to gather about him. It had been a guest-room before the war but now the fripperies had been removed and the tall windows were stark with gas-proof screens. He looked suddenly older, Robert thought. Now his hair shone with grey, new lines emphasized the hardness of his features. But his voice was unchanged, harsh, imperious.

"Gentlemen! The show's to-morrow." He paused and looked slowly at the circle of pilots. "The target you know. Here's the latest from Intelligence and a few other little details I want you to know."

Robert heard his instructions and memorized

them with an ease born of practice, but the words seemed meaningless, rattling like hail on the roof of his mind.

"Any questions?"

But they were all old hands and no naïve youngsters among them wanted to make themselves heard.

"Well . . . good luck! I know you'll put up a good show," his voice was suddenly shy, "I wish they'd let me come with you."

They went back to the ante-room, went on talking, reading, playing the Chinese game. Robert sat down by a friend. They had been together for years but were in different squadrons.

"If anything," Robert's voice was quiet as he flipped the pages of a magazine, "if anything were . . . to slip up . . . to-morrow, would you attend to the odd detail?"

"Of course, old boy." The other puffed his pipe alight, swung the match till it was extinguished.

"To-morrow?"

"Yes."

"Tough show?"

"Tough enough."

. . . . .

It was almost day as Robert walked over to

Flights with the Squadron Leader, and cold with the half light lying dead on the roofs of the camouflaged hangars and the wind-sock flapping drearily on its pole. The erks were beginning to start up the motors, which clattered protestingly to life, back-firing and juddering on their bearers.

"Looks like a good day, sir?"

The leader of the raid looked up, then kicked his heel into the turf. "Yes: hope this frost holds off. I hope to hunt next week." It was a lot too clear, Robert thought. He hoped there was more cloud over there.

"You got some leave, sir?"

"Yes, I'm lucky. Six days."

"I'll say you're lucky." Not too much cloud, he thought, covering the target and only too likely to be full of ice this time of year.

"Have you been out with the local pack?" the older man went on.

"No, I can't get anyone to mount me." He wondered if they'd have any of the new twin fighters waiting for them. They hadn't been seen yet, and were supposed to be very fast and to carry cannons.

"That *is* the trouble," said the Squadron Leader. When Robert got to his machine only the starboard engine had been started. Impatiently he watched the efforts of the crew. If only they'd get that engine running, he thought, if only they'd get it running. If only they'd get it running. He went up to the fitter.

"You haven't over-doped?"

"No, sir. She'll go now."

Still she refused to start. He climbed up the ladder into the cockpit.

"Got your throttle setting right?"

"Yes, sir," said the Corporal, "she'll start in a minute."

The Second Pilot was inside, busy at the navigator's table.

"All set?" Robert asked.

"Bombs, petrol and everything hunkey dorey, sir," the Sergeant answered.

If only they'd start that engine, he thought, if only they'd get it going and we could take off.

At last the motor roared to life and he climbed into his seat, ran up the engines, pulled up the ladder and waved away the chocks.

As he waited on the aerodrome, his airscrews throwing long flickering shadows, he kicked the heavy rudder violently from side to side. Where were the others? Where were the others? They would be late off the ground and there'd be a row. Then he glanced at his watch and found to his surprise that it was five minutes to zero hour. Behind him the wireless operator was hidden by his tall set and the gunners were amidships waiting to take up their positions once the machine was airborne. The Second Pilot leaned over the navigating table, setting his maps and charts and instruments.

And now the other machines were taxi-ing towards him, huge heavily laden monoplanes, grim against the dawn, moving fast over the close-cut turf, beating down clean thick lines through the white frost. He glanced down at the controls, felt the various cocks, checked the cylinder-head temperatures, the hydraulic and brake pressures. Then, when all was ready, he pushed open the throttles, the noise increasing till it filled the long narrow compartment, beating mercilessly upon his ears, drowning the scream of the hydraulic gear.

She was heavy with full petrol and a belly full of bombs, but as he felt her becoming airborne he brought the wheel gently back and she bumped up into the air.

. . . . .

They flew in tight formation and far below patches of fog lay pressed into the valleys. The sun threw skinny shadows, exaggerating the place of the leafless trees in the landscape, and blue smoke rose in stiff columns from farm chimneys, a bitter blue against the slight haze. Looking down at this scene of unreal cleanness Robert found it hard to believe it was War. This is an exercise, he thought, Redland against Blueland, and we shall meet the "enemy" fighter pilots in Mess to-night and have a terrific party.

As they approached the coast he noticed a familiar seaside town to the north. It was lifeless now, the blatant lettering on every house and shop and hoarding screaming to empty streets, to deserted beaches and amusement parks: it was garish in the clear early light, like the face of a prostitute as she slips out in the morning to buy food.

The sea was calm, edged with white froth. The calm was a good thing, he thought, for the rubber dinghy they carried in the wing was not designed to weather a gale.

Always before, the coast had been the meeting-place of land and sea, a convenient opportunity for obtaining a navigational "fix" or position. But now, as he glanced at the little boats askew on the beaches like burnt matches on a bar floor, he thought, "This is the edge of England." Then he looked ahead at the hard cold grey of the North Sea and edged a little closer to the Squadron Leader's aircraft.

. . . . .

From time to time Robert switched on his microphone and spoke to each gunner in his turret. They were alert and cheerful and behind him the Second Pilot worked at his check navigation, taking sights, drifts, bearings, his face expressionless, his movements slow and sure so that he might have been in a classroom.

Sometimes they saw fishing-boats whose crews waved frantically, and tiny minesweepers busy at their deadly task and once a convoy with destroyers like sheepdogs on its flanks. The weather was fine, with high lumps of cumulus, and they began to climb.

In a little while the Second Pilot came forward and held up eight fingers. Robert nodded. Eight minutes. He felt cold inside his guts, his teeth were chattering, he wished they were in the thick of it, and grinned at his companion. The target came into view, a smudge on the horizon. The

Leader began to give his orders over the radio and they started a big circle so as to attack from out of the sun. As they came up the sky filled with anti-aircraft fire. The Second Pilot had switched on his microphone and Robert could hear him jeering at the enemy gunners, for the shooting was poor, though some of the bursts were uncomfortably close.

They came over the target and released their bombs. Robert watched the sky unceasingly for enemy fighters, turning a little and holding up his thumb against the sun, squinting round the edge of the glove, wondering if any aircraft were lurking in its glare waiting for the anti-aircraft to cease before diving to the attack.

The Second Pilot was busy with the camera recording the hits far below, whistling as he worked. A burst of Archie off the port wing-tip made the machine rock violently. The Second Pilot kept absolutely motionless for a few seconds. Robert looked out along the wing where little strips of fabric were fluttering back from the leading edge but the machine still flew perfectly and he moved the wheel gingerly, grinning as the ailerons responded. The Second Pilot turned slowly back to his task.

Soon they were out of range of the ground guns and Robert saw one of the other machines break formation and rock its wings. He spoke to the gunners.

"Keep your eyes skinned. There's a fighter about somewhere." Then he saw it, a lone enemy machine, a single-seat fighter with square wing-tips. It came up quite slowly, lazily, flying on to the tail of one of the bombers. It was so simple a manœuvre that it might have been a pupil on his circuit at a flying training-school. As it turned off, short jabs of black smoke jerked themselves from the back cockpit of the bomber. The fighter turned slowly on to its side. First smoke, then flames, poured from its engine, splashing down the fuselage. In the bright sunshine, against the blue sea, the flames were orange, and the machine fell slowly, twisting, turning, diving.

"Here they come!" said the Second Pilot, and Robert saw that the sky seemed to be filled with fighters. They broke up and began to attack. Robert watched two circling him from the front. As they turned the flank his rear gunner switched on his microphone and Robert could hear him swearing. He used one obscene word after another. They were meaningless, uttered without expression, repeated over and over again like the rhyme of a child. Tracer from the enemy streamed overhead, curved in graceful trajectory and dropped out of sight. Then the gunner was silent. Robert heard the rattle of his guns and his voice, jubilant.

"Got him, sir."

"Good. Keep your eyes skinned."

The middle gunner reported a machine. "But he's yellow, sir. Keeps out of range."

"Be patient," Robert said.

Now a twin-engined aircraft came up on the beam, accompanied by one of the smaller fighters, which attacked from the rear. A burst of fire shattered the roof over the Second Pilot's head. The front gunner coolly brought his guns to bear. The twin was an ugly brute, the first Robert had seen with extended stabilizers on the tail. He was frightened now, his mouth dry, his hands wet inside the silk lining of his gloves.

The gunners reported unceasingly. They were flying at full throttle and Robert looked despairingly ahead for cloud, but the nearest cumulus was miles away. Attack after attack came up, filled the air with tracer, turned lazily away. The middle gunner brought down another fighter before he was hit in the leg. Robert sent the Second Pilot back in his place.

One burst of machine-gun-fire shattered half the instrument panel, sent a shower of broken glass over his knees. Darkness filled his eyes, but in his mind he could still see the face of the enemy gunner, red and foolishly grim as he fired from the rear cockpit of the fighter. The wheel went limp in his hands, the strain of months of war, the nag of responsibility, lifted from his consciousness. This is good, he thought, this is good. To relax, to relax, to relax.

Then his vision cleared and he pulled the aircraft level. To his surprise the fighters had vanished and at his side was the Squadron Leader's machine, which he thought he had seen go down. The enemy must have run out of ammunition. He began to sing, thumping his hands on the wheel.

. . . . .

They were separated from the others and flew in tight formation, the Squadron Leader turning his head from time to time and grinning and doing a thumbs up. They lost height till they were just above the sea, their patterned shadows sliding effortlessly over mile after mile of watery desolation. On crossing the coast the Senior Officer altered course for base. They flew at a few hundred feet over the sleepy countryside, their shadows now vaulting hedge and haystack, silently, climbing ridge and col, dropping easily into shallow valleys.

The sun was still high in the sky and the country had never been more lovely. Not pretty, Robert thought, in the frills of summer, but beautiful in the starkness of winter. As he looked, first to the north at the black rich earth of the ferns, marshalled by dykes, then south to the flatness of Suffolk, woolly with leaf-stripped trees, each feature of the country fitted into its place in his mind, each town he knew, hazy and grey with the mist of a winter's afternoon, each stretch of river, pregnant now with flood, each change of character from county to county. How familiar, he thought. How well I know it all. Truly, England is my village.

. . . . .

Soon the little lake shaped like an elephant's trunk appeared and they dived low over the hangars, then broke away, dropped their wheels and came in to land. There were no other machines about and the camp seemed strangely deserted.

A little later they walked into the Mess. It was warm and comfortable in there and the words and phrases of the many conversations jumbled themselves into a haze of sound. At the table by the fire there was an empty chair at the Chinese game. When Robert saw the other players he stopped in his stride. There was Nails, who got his on the first show, and Dick, who went down in flames, and Thistle his second pilot, and Badger, who was lost in the North Sea in December.

"Come on!" Badger said. "We're waiting for you."

"But I thought . . ." Robert said. "I thought . . ."

Badger was smiling.

# The Man who was Dead

# The Man who was Dead

Although I was only a child at the time, the memory of him in the picturesque uniform of the Royal Flying Corps has never faded in my mind. My father was the parson and the Vicarage bounded on the Manor, so that we children all played together; games of Indians and Trappers and Explorers and Hunters, playing with that grimness and aggressive self-assertion of childhood that we like to forget when we grow older and become adult in body.

Ray was the eldest of the Squire's scatter-brained family and he used to roar with refreshing unexpectedness into our little world. Sometimes he was in a frail contrivance of silver, brave with Royal Flying Corps markings, that dipped and circled the chimneys, the regular stutter of its motor bringing the villagers out of their cottages, for it was not often that one saw an aircraft in 1917, frightening the stock on the village green, stampeding us children out of nursery or shrubbery into a silent worshipping group on one of the lawns.

At other times he appeared in a stripped racing-car, more than ever a god to us, with jauntily set forage-cap, ragged, oil-stained flying coat over the trim "maternity jacket" they wore in those days, his fingers yellow with tobacco smoke. (And now, if someone mentions his name, the picture comes swiftly to my mind, the tiny fair moustache, the pink cheeks and curly hair, the regular features still characterless, the speech the platitudes of a schoolboy, clothed in a charming stammer.)

He spoilt us all, remembering our names and fancies, bought us the outrageously expensive sweets and toys and poorly printed books of the time, unashamedly enjoying our excitement. A little while after this he went to France to one of the famous Fighter Squadrons, shooting down several of the enemy before he himself was brought down in flames to spend the rest of the war in hospital.

When he returned they made a fuss of him in

the village. There was a reception, I remember, at the parish hall, with a tea thrown in, and my father and the doctor made speeches while he stood, supported by two sticks, on the stage. He made the conventional speech, but his smile had no kindliness in it, his tones were bored and that evening I heard Cook telling my nurse that the Squire's son was drinking "something awful".

Afterwards I went away to be very unhappy at a public school, and in the holidays when I played with Ray's brothers I understood, from a dropped remark, a sidelong glance, a half-finished sentence, a frown from an elder sister, that there were money troubles and that Ray, who had failed in a garage venture, refused to work, but claimed to be "looking after the estate" and was running up debts in neighbouring towns and drinking more heavily than ever. He had become such a black sheep that his family were almost proud of him.

Sometimes my father, or a relation, would ask me what I wanted to do in life, and I would always answer without hesitation, "become an airman". Then my father would smile and tell me a story of a country boy who went to sea, his imagination fired by a picture at home of a beautiful sailing-ship on a tropic, placid sea. But I used to laugh, being sure with the untried confidence of youth, and felt sorry for my father, who, I felt, knew so little. And as I laughed I thought of a little fighter 'plane, starred with bullet-holes, the tattered fabric fluttering in little streams from the wings as I dived and rolled and looped, seeing my face, framed by a flying helmet and topped by Meyrowitz goggles, mirrored in the air-speed indicator, the earth tilting and swinging below, hearing the cry of the wind in the wires, feeling the slipstream leaning on my face. For I met Ray from time to time and our talk was always of flying.

At first he would be loath to speak, muttering that this shop would bore me, but as I insisted he would begin to talk of the old days, of training in the Flying Corps in England and flying with the legendary heroes in France. And then he would forget himself and there would be light in his eyes again and the words would tumble one on the next as they had used to do, his drawl a thing forgotten.

. . . . .

It was dusk as we came back from the raid. We had fought off a series of attacks by enemy fighters and one of my flight had gone down. I felt bad about it in an abstract fashion, for war drives home the place of chance in life, and against my judgement I found myself sentimentalizing about the captain, who was an old friend of mine. I was seeking in my mind for the subject we had been chatting about as we went up to Flights from the operations room that morning, trying to remember what he last did in my presence that I, with the kindness of sentiment, might clothe his last actions in dignity, endow his last speech with wisdom.

The navigator came forward with a map in his hand and peered down into the grey evening. The other member of my show rode at my wing-tip, a big black shape, sinister in the half light, rising and falling as he hit the bumps, but never losing close formation, his red navigation light like an evil eye in the approaching night. Little tongues of flame licked out of his exhaust stubs. I was tired, my clothes were damp with sweat under my Irvin and I could smell the cordite from the gun-turrets that still lingered in the machine. The rotten taste of oxygen was in my mouth.

Soon the navigator put up his thumb and pointed. The aerodrome was on the port bow. I altered course. Switching on my microphone I spoke to the crew. The wireless operator wound in his aerial, the gunners came out of their turrets. One of them was holding his arm, which was bound with bloodstained emergency dressing. When I glanced anxiously at him he grinned and put up his thumb. I would have liked to have shot up the camp, but we had a few holes that might be in stressed parts, so we flew low over the Mess and the groups of troops and workmen and Mess waiters and officers who were awaiting our return, dropped our wheels and flaps and landed.

It was some time before I left the operations room and walked slowly to the Mess with the pilot who had flown by my side for eight hours. He was a young Canadian and excitement and relief had quickened his slow Alberta speech. As we entered the foyer I could hear the sound of a party in the ante-room.

"That'll be the concert bunch," my companion said. "It's Thursday. They've been giving the troops a show."

"Of course," I said. "It's Thursday."

For out there is neither day nor night, nor winter nor summer, only light and darkness, heat and cold. One is either alive or dead, filled with hope or despair. One is laughing or crying. Now I was back in the real world of God and right and wrong and patriotism and money. "Of course," I said, "it's Thursday."

We went in and I sat down in a corner. There was a terrific row going on. The male entertainers wore unbuttoned, double-breasted dinner-jackets, which displayed, usually, a gaudy pullover. The girls had too much make-up on and looked tired and in need of a rest and a good meal. Everyone was making a great deal of noise in their determination to be cheerful. All the guests were drinking Pimms and singing and whistling through their teeth.

Then somebody saw us and in an instant the party was forgotten and we were surrounded. What had happened? Did we get there? What damage did we do? What happened to Jimmy? Was the anti-aircraft bad? Were there many fighters up?"

"We got there," I said.

"Any luck?"

"Yes. As far as I could see we blew the place to hell."

"Anti-aircraft?"

"Not bad," the young Canadian said. "Made the air a bit bumpy at times!"

"And fighters?"

"Not so hot," I said. "But one of them got a lucky shot in."

"Jimmy?"

"Yes."

"What happened?" The voices were quiet now, almost casual.

"He was flying in tight formation with us for about a minute, with flames coming out of his turrets. Then he went slap into the drink."

"Anybody get out?"

"No," I said.

"That's tough. Young Smith was his second dicky, wasn't he?"

"Yes," I said. I looked round the ante-room. One always found it hard to believe that one had been hundreds of miles over the sea, into an enemy country, fought a battle and returned. One had a feeling of leaving the Mess and then coming back into it again. It was the real and the unreal. "It's tough," I said.

"It's tough," echoed in my mind. It just meant he was dead and wouldn't come into Mess any more. It just meant you lied and told his Missus you thought he was a prisoner of war. Through it all the familiar ring: "*It can't be so hard. . . . It can't be so hard*". Suddenly someone began to play the piano, the singing and whistling began again, a drink was pushed into my hand.

I talked to a blonde for a while. Underneath the make-up that deadened her features she had an interesting, intelligent face; but as she spoke she watched one of her companions, a seedy youngster who was tipsy and playing the piano very badly.

In a far corner was a new-comer to the Mess. He was one of the older officers who were taking over the ground jobs, held a very junior rank but had wings above his Pip, Squeak and Wilfred. I watched him for some time before I realized it was Ray, an older, fatter Ray. His neck was very red and bulged over his collar. His eyes were glassy. I waved to him and he came quickly to my side. When we had talked a little he looked shyly at my stripes.

"I suppose I ought to call you 'Sir'?"

"Don't be an idiot," I said.

The drunken pianist began to play a song about hanging washing on the Siegfried Line. A sudden silence fell upon the crowded room, for songs like these are not popular among men who fight. The boy at the piano, oblivious of the faint disapproval about him, played on and on, lifting his hands high above the keys, sometimes striking a wrong note, happy as the central figure in a world of his own imagining.

"You've been on a show to-day?" Ray asked.

"Yes," I said.

"Hear you lost a machine?"

"Yes," I said.

He drained his beer at a gulp. "It's good to be back."

"Have a drink?"

"Thanks, I will."

The waiter grinned as I ordered and said he was glad to see me back. I asked Ray about his people. They were all well, he said. The blonde girl went over to the piano and took the boy away. She began to play herself, some classical stuff. It had a kick in it and she played it well, sitting stiffly, one shoulder a little higher than the other.

"I had a look at one of your machines to-day," Ray said. "They're very complicated, aren't they?"

"Not really, just a mass of gadgets you soon get used to."

"I suppose you're right." He drank deeply, then looked up at me with eyebrows raised. "It's a lot different, you know, from my day."

"I suppose it is."

"There isn't . . . well, it's just different."

"Yes," I said.

The Wing Commander came in and talked to me for a while. I introduced him to Ray. Ray began to talk. He called the senior officer "sir" too often. Kept on referring to the '14–'18 campaign. Then the Old Man drifted away. I took Ray round and introduced him to the Squadron. "Nice lot of lads," he'd say as we walked from one group to another. "Nice lot of lads. We still have the stuff."

As I stood by the piano roaring out the old songs, I watched him drifting from group to group, talking a little too much, laughing a little too loudly, a little too insistent in his self-depreciation, bragging, exaggerating, so delighted with himself that he had no hesitation in butting into any conversation, so eager to buy a round.

At last, when he had been politely elbowed out of every little clique, he went over to a group of the entertainers and I watched him as he stood in a circle of them. He had bought a round of Pimms and they were all listening eagerly to what he had to say.

# Ice

# Ice

The next evening we started night flying and when I landed at one o'clock Moira was waiting with her car in the shadow of the duty pilot's hut.

She smiled at my protests. I was happy and very tired. The engines still pounded in my ears and my eyes were sore with the strain of peering through the darkness. We drove through the camp and down the road. Chuck droned overhead, his navigation lights floating smoothly through the stillness. Moira looked upwards. There was high cloud, hard in the moonlight. The last of the searchlights to the south swung stiffly over the sky.

"Isn't it lonely up there?"

"Sometimes."

"I don't like being lonely . . . it frightens me and I hate being frightened."

I smiled at her and touched her arm.

"What have you to be frightened of?"

"Oh, lots of things."

"Such as?"

"Oh, being ill . . . and things. And, of course, women's fear . . . of growing old."

"I'm afraid of growing old, too," I said.

"You?"

"Yes."

"But I never thought——"

"That men . . .?"

"Your lives aren't in your bodies . . . you've jobs and comradeship and things. . . ."

"Think of children," I said, "and the common delusion that they have ideal lives. But as you know, it's a time of frustration, of physical disadvantage, a period of uncontrolled emotion, intolerance, thoughtlessness and untried confidence. As you grow into a man you lose all these things, gain a wider, better life. But when age comes, you begin to die and live in the past, you get careful, your body begins to let you down, you can't drink and fight and make love like you used to . . . you're on the way back again. I hate the thought of it."

"You love life . . . don't you, Paul?"

"I think it's grand," I said.

"And you don't fear death?"

"Not really, I suppose."

"At one time I used to despise your sort of life . . . now I'm not at all sure."

I was beginning to get warm again and thinking of the party that would be beginning soon at the Blue Boar, how we would laugh and drink through the night.

"You haven't forgotten about your promise?"

"Which one, darling?"

"To take me up at night!"

"If you really want to go?"

"I do."

"Then Friday?"

"That'll be lovely." She began to hum, beating time on the wheel with a small gloved hand.

Friday was a bad flying day, grey and cold with heavy cumulus building up to great heights. I rang up Moira's hotel after tea but she had already left and as I did my last joy-ride I saw her car creeping over the rough ground at the edge of the flying field.

"I tried to get you on the 'phone," I said. "It's not going to be much good for flying to-night."

"Are they going to cancel it?"

"You don't catch 'em washing it out if they can get off the ground," Jack said, "not when they're paid well by the hour."

"Well, what's the trouble?" Moira asked.

"Everything's on the top line," I said, "but I'd rather take you up some time when you could see a bit more."

"You're going up to-night, aren't you?"

"Yes."

"Then I'd like to go too."

We got into the car and drove through the quiet evening, rain splattering on the windscreen. We passed cyclists heading into the weather and groups of visitors in bedraggled holiday clothes, waiting for buses, and buses themselves, their windows steamed with breath. As we went by a favourite pub of mine Moira looked at me, her mouth twisting into a smile.

"If you'd like a drink, I'll wait."

"I don't drink before night shows."

"Really?"

"Yes. My father was the same and his father before him."

Stopping before we reached the Royal Air Force station we used as a base, Moira pulled a white flying-suit over her beach clothes and covered her hair with an old flying helmet.

"You're quite an aviator," I said, and kissed her.

"Darling! Won't there be dreadful trouble if I'm caught?"

"You worry too much," I said. "Who's going to catch us?"

The sentry knew me and I drove through the camp, cheerless and windswept, to the hangar we used to house our aircraft. I helped Moira into my machine and sent a mechanic off for an indemnity form.

"You must sign this, just put your initials and surname."

"What is it?"

"A blood chit . . . means your people can't claim if I kill you to-night."

"Then the firm know I'm flying?"

"Yes . . . they've got your sex wrong . . . that's all."

I went out to the flare path to find the chief pilot, as the programme had been altered. How familiar it all was! The airmen grouped about the first flare, silhouetted against the brazier as medieval soldiers about a camp-fire, the gay navigation fights of the aircraft circling the aerodrome as goldfish in a bowl.

And when a machine came in to land, the lights growing brighter as they sank quietly towards one, the muttered conversations would die away and one would hear only the thrash of the airscrews, the rattle of throttled motors, the rhythmic click of the signalling-lamp, the wind whispering over the short grass, the hoot of an owl, the patient chimes of the church clock.

Again the old magic recaptured one, the acrid smell of a coke brazier and paraffin flares, the laconic speech of riggers and fitters, laced with obscenity, floating over from the hangars.

Suddenly the 'plane, seeming to accelerate violently and to grow to gargantuan proportions, bumps to rest up the flare path with a hollow rumbling, the engine cowlings gleaming in the malleable light.

Receiving my instructions I returned to my machine and started up the engines. As I waited for them to warm up I tested the wireless, plugging Moira's telephones into the circuit. When the oil was warm enough I pushed each throttle open in turn, testing the dual ignition system on each engine, watching maximum revolutions and boost pressure. To my companion, who sat with head bowed and hands gripping the edge of the seat, it was simply a huge wave of sound, enveloping her mind, beating upon her ears.

She would find terror in the mighty power of the engine as it strained at the bearers and rocked the whole machine, while the slipstream beat across the tarmac and swirled dust and oddments into the hangar. But to me, mind hungry with anticipation, emotion brittle with experience, it was something more, the sheer noise subordinate to the idea that dominated my consciousness.

As I taxied out I saw the signaller at the first flare test his Aldis lamp by flashing it on the ground and a little later a green "M" splashed over the machine. I came up to the bottom of the path, checking switches and petrol-cocks in the darkness, each detail pigeon-holed in my mind. I thought of nothing, custom and dexterity were carrying me with them. Another green fell across my tail and I let off the brakes and opened up my engines.

Bumping down the flare path I was ham on the rudder as the aircraft had a pronounced swerve. The wheel too was heavy in my hands after hundreds of hours on light aeroplanes.

Gradually she became airborne and then the last flare disappeared and I was flying in blackness, seeing nothing. I bent back my head and looked through the roof at the stars. But they were only partly visible and no guide as to whether I was flying level. I throttled down and changed the airscrews into coarse, climbing on the airspeed till the gyro began to work. Then it was easy, and I went up through three thousand feet of cloud, heading for my first run.

When we came out of the clouds it was clear above. I could hear Chuck on the wireless, reporting his position, and as I watched, the searchlights got him like a moth caught by a flashlight on the ceiling, a tiny white 'plane thousands of feet above.

Below the world was stifled with darkness, all life stilled by the blanket of night which enveloped the earth. Occasionally a light, growing out of the blackness, would float towards us till it dipped beneath a wing and was lost. I used to wonder about these islands in a quiet world, think of them as quiet homes and happy crowds in pubs (as a lonely youth, seeing man and woman walking together, thinks of them as lovers, imagines a strange intimacy to exist between them).

We turned over the town which formed the western limit of my run. Climbing still I looked down, watching cars pushing little cylinders of light along the roads, and the town itself, a thing of beauty, with regular illuminations of many colours.

At ten thousand feet I turned off my navigation lights and started on my first run, reporting to base as I ruddered red on red. Chuck, hearing me, chipped in.

"Hullo, Paul, you old so-and-so."

"Hullo, Chuck . . . what's the weather like with you?"

"Nothing striking . . . there's some goosh coming up from the south."

"Where are you?"

"Twelve zero zero zero, flying a little west of north from Swanmouth."

"What could you do to a drink?"

"I hope they leave enough for us."

The operator at base ticked us off for talking and I flew on in silence. Cloud was forming far below and I had been up for three-quarters of an hour before the searchlights got me, filling the cabin with blinding purple light. I half-closed my eyes and flew on the gyro. Then the clouds intervened, sucking up the strong light as blotting-paper ink and leaving me in loneliness once more.

In a little while the cloud had completely covered the ground and lay as snow, peaceful and motionless, in the moonlight. Base ordered me to return and turning on the navigation lights I started to glide down, flying on dead reckoning.

The clouds came slowly up to meet us. Moira pointed down delightedly. I opened up both motors to warm them. Without warning, the port engine coughed and cut. I pulled out the tiny flashlamp I carried stuck under my tie and checked the cocks. They were correctly set and there was plenty of petrol. I leaned over and pulled out my companion's telephones, then called up base, telling them what had happened, asking for rockets so that I could find the aerodrome quickly when I got down through the thick stuff.

I closed the starboard engine and dived into the clouds. In a flash the calm beauty vanished. It was bumpy and hailing, and I fought to keep her on her course. The cloud gleamed white in the light of the small headlight I had turned on, while rain and hail swished rhythmically in the starboard airscrew. Ice began to build up on the windscreen, slapping across the glass as a wet floor-cloth on stone flags.

Now I watched the starboard airscrew in the light of the top identification light to see if it was icing up. The next time I glanced at the airspeed the needle had flickered back to zero as the Pitot head was now frozen up.

I glanced at Moira, but she seemed unperturbed. The gyro, on which I was now flying, was Venturi operated. The Venturi tube was almost certainly ice-coated and in a few minutes the instrument would be useless.

I rocked the stick laterally, watching for lag on the gyro. There was enormous depth to this violent self-contained storm and a Whippet, having a flat glide, took a long time to get through. Gradually the tiny horizon, which was now my sole guide, moved more and more slowly, till it dropped away from the small replica of an aircraft. The gyro was no longer working.

Now I was powerless, having no indication of what the machine was doing. She began to dive steeply, the wind whistling in the half-opened window. I hauled back on the stick and lurched over to Moira, who was white with terror.

Grinning, I shoved on opposite bank. I became

conscious that the machine was standing on its tail, the controls losing effect. The altimeter needle was down to the two thousand mark. I began to get frightened. It was the old familiar sensation, as a dream well known, half fanciful, shadowing the mind as one lies half awake.

First my mouth grew dry and there was a cold empty feeling in my guts. I was conscious of the palms of my hands sticky with sweat, of my shirt clinging to my back. My teeth were chattering. Let me get out this time, I thought, let me get out with this woman I love. Let me get out this time and I'll stop drinking, I'll behave my bloody self. Let me get out this time and I'll never be unhappy again . . . it'll be enough just to be alive.

Again it was clear to me that the object of life was to continue living and my mind, quickened by fear, began to notice insignificant things, a loose screw in the corner of the dashboard, the pattern of shadow thrown by the top identification light on to my companion's flying-suit.

At a thousand feet we came out of the clouds. I saw some lights above my left shoulder and wrenched the machine over, putting the starboard airscrew into fine and opening up the engine. The controls were very stiff, but whether from ice or speed I could not tell. Despite the override, we were losing height, so I decided to land and pulled off a parachute reconnaissance flare.

The blinding light lit up the countryside, and shielding my eyes with a wing I searched for a field. In a little while I saw what looked like a pasture, with approaches free of trees. I throttled back and did an approach, pulling up the nose to lose height. At the critical moment the flare went out. I tried to hold the shape of what lay underneath in my mind and switched on the landing-lamp, shouting to Moira to walk aft. But she paid no attention, sitting still by my side. Then I saw the dark line of the fence and knew that I was much too high. The Whippet was a low-wing monoplane and was popularly supposed to be impossible to sideslip.

"You bastard!" I said, and put on fifty degrees of bank, kicking up the nose with top rudder. I was very scared.

The machine fell sideways, the slipstream screaming in the open window at my ear. As I pulled out I saw the hedge in front. My heart jumped inside me, for I had already switched off. I pulled the stick back hard and then let it forward as we cleared the obstacle. We hit the ground with a bang that sent my head hard against the roof. Then we bounced and I waited for the crunch as we came down again but she bumped and swerved up the field to a standstill.

Moira was sobbing and holding my arm.

"Is your head all right?" I asked.

"My head's all right," she said, "my head's all right," and went on repeating the phrase till it became meaningless. I got out and inspected the damage, which amounted to torn fabric, broken tail wheel, burst tyre, and buckled oleo leg. When I climbed back into the cabin Moira was quiet. She clung to my arm again. Her hands were trembling.

"I was so sure . . . so sure . . . I knew your world . . . but dear God . . . I didn't know it was this."

Far away to the north-west a rocket went up, turning slowly earthwards as it reached the clouds, like a burnt match in the sky.

# Too Young to Live

E

# Too Young to Live

It was some time before the youngster with the broken back realized that he was going to die.

He was placed in the bed next to mine and at first they used to pump him full of dope so that he lay lifeless, body caged in nineteen pounds of plaster, mind smothered with narcotics. We saw but little of him, only a glimpse of a stiff body, even beneath the sheets, and a white face topped with black hair, seen when they moved the screens; or heard a groan or murmur or half-stifled sob in the long bleak night. Truth to tell, I rather think we resented his arrival with something of that umbrage which railway passengers adopt when a late traveller invades their carriage, as if our being together for a little while had given us a peculiar fellowship we were loath to lose.

This was accentuated by the attention he needed, for the ward orderlies watched him constantly, Sister looked in every few minutes and Senior Medical officers were often at his bedside.

The mild Spring weather was vile that year, incessant rain beating on the tall ugly windows and low broken cloud drifting swiftly a few hundred feet above. Only occasionally did it clear and the shy sunshine fell in patches on the panorama that stretched out to Oxfordshire, pale and green and lovely with the new crops breaking through the warm earth.

The nights were worse than the days, for in the quiet darkness the huge hospital seemed like a gagged beast and I would lie awake and think of all the mute suffering around me, and steel myself not to look at my watch, and listen to the far-away sound of the rain, and be afraid to die, and wonder how much night flying the boys were doing and whether I should ever fly again.

When Night Sister tiptoed away from the youngster I would sometimes call softly to her and she would come swiftly to my bedside and look sternly at me and ask me why I wasn't asleep, and I would grin and plead for more "knock-out shot", as we called sleeping draught. But she would smile and switch off my shaded lamp, put away my book, smooth my pillow and tell me to lie quietly and wait for sleep to come. She was graceful and quick, with pain-knowing hands, moving with swish of starched apron, cool and certain in her actions, womanly sympathy ousted by the ability to lessen suffering, an automaton produced by perfect training and experience.

Occasionally, when the dim light of the night bulbs fell kindly on her features, I would catch a glimpse of lost beauty far beyond youthfulness that was shining through the passing of the years and would hold my breath at the thought of it, thinking of her as a girl, mischievous as laughter bubbled on her mouth, forgetting that she was now close-hauled to forty and unpopular with the others, who called her "the old geyser" and alleged that the decoration ribbon she wore belonged to a Zulu war medal.

Martin was one of the worst offenders in this respect. He too was my neighbour and also suffered from insomnia. We used to smoke a lot in the nights and the tips of our cigarettes would make steady rhythmic arcs in the darkness. He had been brought down by Wogs on the North-West Frontier and was a long time recovering from his injuries. Women, and particularly Night Sister, infuriated him and the orderlies who served under her earned his contempt for obeying her orders. Sometimes we talked quietly, but usually lay silent, for he said but little, living every moment as he came to it, as a good pilot should, remembering little of what had passed, having no dread of the future. His passion was for news, and when the little old newspaperman came round each morning he would buy half a dozen papers, fold them carefully and read each one from cover to cover, an operation which took him most of the day. Yet he would remember little of what he had read and his contributions to heated arguments were conventional to ludicrousness.

The little old newspaperman, whose coming was the brightest event in the morning and who cashed our cheques and ran our errands, made the same joke each morning. "Better orf in 'ere, gents," he would say as he shuffled down the ward. "Better orf in 'ere than outside this weather, gents, you believe me!" But when the youngster had been in a day or two the old man must have realized something of what lay behind those screens, for he joked no more but passed quickly from bed to bed, clinking the shining cylinder of pennies he held in his left hand; a little twisted figure to whom age had brought no dignity, eager to run at the whim of any supercilious whelp with a penny to spend, a man to whom life had brought no more than degradation of caste.

. . . . .

After three days the youngster drifted back to life, and when the Medical Officer came round I heard him speak, asking the doctor how bad he was and how long it would take for him to be well and when he would be able to fly again. I was frightened by the elder man's reply as he raised his eyebrows to the Senior Sister, for in those mechanical tones that carried so easily the assurance of early recovery and the explanation of partial paralysis being due to shock, there was, it seemed to me, a hideousness of false hope, a cruelty of misrepresentation that surpassed even the tragedy itself.

Then he asked that the screens should be taken away, and when the doctor had gone one of the orderlies, Hopkins, the good-looking lad who knew all the latest smut and backed horses for us, came and took them away. We watched with interest, Martin and I and the kid who had flown into a hillside, and the Canadian who hit a tree night flying, and the two appendicitis cases, and the Squadron Leader who had broken his arm during a Guest Night. This was something new, an object of interest in our measured day. The other milestones we knew, the early tea, chilled and half in saucer, the washing of patients, the bed making, the floor polishing, the visit of the newspaperman, the flowers brought in, the eagerly awaited mealtimes. This was different, an unexpected tit-bit.

He lay very still for a while, blinking in the sunshine, seemingly oblivious of the interest of nine patients. Then in a little while he twisted his head and looked at me. I grinned.

"Good morning," I said.

"Good morning, sir."

"You don't call me 'Sir'. . . . How d'you feel, anyhow?"

"I'm . . . much better . . . thanks."

"You've come on well . . ." I said.

"Yes . . . I felt pretty grim at first."

"You'll soon be all right again now. . . ."

"Yes . . . I'll soon be . . . all right again . . . now."

I had a little mirror mounted on the radiator at my bedside so that I could watch the reflection of aeroplanes passing overhead. Often I would look up from my book and catch a glimpse of aircraft (how easy and simple it seemed and how difficult to imagine the rain prickling one's face and the machines rising and falling on either side as they hit the bumps and one's map sodden on one's knee and low clouds ahead fringed with angry rain). And I would follow the flight unheeding, my mind still busy with my book so that the passage of the machine would be incorporated in some part of it, woven in its essential fabric as a scene sometimes interpolates itself into a conversation, bits of countryside linking themselves illogically to the sequence of the words.

As I idly watched a big bomber moving with stately indifference through the base of the clouds, sometimes growing grey and misty, occasionally disappearing altogether, I heard the youngster's voice.

"Is that a Moose, sir?"

"Yes," I said, "it's a Moose."

"Have you flown them?"

I nodded.

"They must be grand to fly!"

"They're all right," I said.

"I suppose you've flown a lot of types?"

"Well . . . I've flown one or two."

"It must be wonderful . . . to have flown lots . . . I mean . . . and to have done hundreds and hundreds of hours."

"You get used to it," I said. "How much have you done?"

"Seven hours dual and twenty-five minutes solo . . . it was on my second solo that . . . it happened."

"That was hard cheese."

"Yes, it does . . . set one back a bit. All the others will leave me far behind now."

"You'll be fine in a few weeks," I said, "and you get the same seniority anyway."

"It's the flying I want."

Then I saw it. Flying to him was an adventure. He belonged to the golden age of the Royal Flying Corps, when aviation was the marvel of mankind and the country was fighting for its life, when every flight was an epic, when every pilot flew in the shadow of death, when the silly breath-taking confidence of youth was in its own, when a pair of wings on one's chest meant that one was more than a pain in the neck to a motor insurance company.

When Night Sister came on duty that evening he was writhing in pain and she shot him full of morphia, holding his hand till the drug crept up like a tide and submerged his pain. He smiled up at her, his face stupid with drowsiness.

"Sorry . . . to make a fuss. Bless you, Sister . . . bless you . . . Sister."

She leaned over him, put his arm beneath the sheets.

"Now you must go to sleep."

He answered so softly that only I could hear.

"Sister!" his voice was thick with sleep.

"What is it?"

"Sister! what's your name?"

She told him her surname.

"No, not that. That's . . . what the others call you . . . what's your real name?"

"Now you mustn't be silly . . . you must go to sleep."

"What's your real name?" He was like a child with its nurse.

"You must go to sleep." Her voice was quiet, as I'd never heard it before.

"You've been so sweet, Sister . . . tell me your real name?"

She whispered so that I couldn't hear.

"Good night, Catherine," he said.

. . . . .

The following morning, listening to our conversation, he seemed a little better, more alive. We talked shop, as usual, of men we knew, machines we had flown, stations in which we'd served. We spoke of crashes and tight corners and hair-raising experiences, bragging by understatement, as the English do. He heard, with eyes shining, the famous Service stories of the fitter who took off to Virginia, the pupil who, following a car to Grantham, spun a Snipe into the ground as he waited for the driver at a cross-roads, of the pilots who have flown beneath the Kenkham bridge, and of the deeds of Batchy Lampgroves and other well-known characters. He listened while we compared an Atlas with a Hart, a Gauntlet with a Super Fury, a Spitfire with a Hurricane, adding no word to our conversation, being content to lie speechless.

That afternoon he began to talk to me again, telling me about his people, who were in India, and how they hated him flying and how his mother had prophesied that his career as a pilot would end in disaster.

"She was . . . sort of fatalistic . . . about it. But she was wrong. I had a pretty good smack, but not as fatal as she thought." It seemed they had a place in England, a house in Suffolk, in the lovely wooded country on the Norfolk border. There was a lot of game there and he wanted me to promise to come up for some shooting. It seemed they thatched with reed rather than wheat straw. "The riding's grand, too; you could have Magpie, and there's bags of hunting and we'd go into market on Wednesday and drink with the farmers and be all friendly with the pubs open all day . . . you'd love it."

"I'll come," I said.

He sighed. "I like it more than any place in the world."

"It's grand country," I said.

"You know it?"

"I've flown over it a lot." As I spoke I could have kicked myself.

"Of course . . . you've flown over it." He was quiet for a little while. Then he said: "I've never seen it from the air myself . . . I always meant to go, but I never got the chance. My instructor wouldn't go very far from the aerodrome."

He could remember every minute of his time in the air, every manœuvre he had been taught, every mistake he had made, every correction, every rebuke, caution or scrap of praise. He never tired of discussing his experiences, little everyday events for the most part that to him had been adventures, glimpses of a new and promised land. As I listened I was amazed, not that he should seem so naïve, but that all I had once felt should now be strange to me, so much enthusiasm be forgotten.

When Night Sister came on duty she went first to the youngster, remarking on the primroses that had just been taken out of the ward.

"They were nice," he said.

"Yes," she answered, "they remind me of home."

"Where's your home, Sister?"

The orderlies brought the screens around his bed and she began to do his dressing, talking quietly, but with unusual fluency, so that the others laid aside their books and headphones to listen.

"It's a long way from here. In a little village in North Wales. My father's the parson there. It's rather grim till you really know it. A grey village in a valley where the sun hardly shines for eight weeks in the winter. It's got tall, hideous chapels and a village shop that sells everything. The hills are all cut with quarries and the houses look very drab with fences of waste slate. But now there are primroses everywhere; it makes it the loveliest time of the year."

When she went out, Martin rolled over towards me.

"I didn't know the old girl was so sentimental, did you?"

"I don't know that she was being particularly sentimental," I said.

"Don't tell me you're getting that way, too!"

"You know me," I said.

. . . . .

I was sleeping better now but the slightest sound still broke the net of my dreams and I awoke a few nights later to hear Night Sister whispering to my neighbour.

"Aren't you asleep yet?"

He must have shaken his head for I heard no reply.

"In pain?"

"N'no."

"Anything you want?"

"Yes . . . stay and talk to me for a bit."

"I can't, I've work to do."

"Oh, Catherine! you're always busy and rushing away . . . can't you stay just a little while?"

"I've told you, and you mustn't . . ."

"Call you Catherine? They're all asleep . . . even he's asleep. . . ." The note of his voice changed as he turned his head towards me.

"Now you must try and sleep yourself."

"You're awfully sweet to me."

She said nothing. In a little while he used her Christian name again.

"Yes, what is it?"

"Catherine . . . you know I'm crazy about you?"

"Don't be a silly boy . . ."

"But I am . . . I've always been . . . since I first came in here."

"You've talked enough foolish things . . . be a good patient and lie still." Her voice was brisk. I heard her pulling his sheets straight. Then she walked past my bed and I watched her as the light caught her face. Her eyes were filled with tears.

. . . . .

The next morning he was much worse and they kept the screens up and told us to be quiet and turned the wireless off and wouldn't let the little old newspaperman sell him a paper. Medical officers came and looked at him every little while and then held long consultations in the Senior

Sister's bunk. It was impossible to understand their mumbled technical jargon, but the orderly who looked after me whispered that the case was quite hopeless.

Then I realized how I hated the place, for suddenly I became aware of the ward, of the sick and smashed men about me, of the smell of ether and floor-polish and radiators and food kept hot in heaters. And more than ever I fretted at the twisted body that held me in bed and wanted to go back to Flights and be with the boys and fly again and get drunk in the nights.

When Night Sister came on duty she stood by his bed for some minutes. Then he recognized her.

"What's . . . the matter . . . Catherine?"

"Nothing . . . we're going to move you into another ward, that's all."

"A private ward?"

"Yes."

He didn't say anything for a long while. Then he whispered, "I guess I had it coming to me."

"What are you talking about?"

"You know," he said.

"You mustn't get silly ideas in your head."

"Catherine?"

"Yes."

"I do love you . . . don't cry, lass."

. . . . .

We never saw him again and the next day a new patient, a young officer injured at rugger, was in his bed. He was very young, very pink-faced, very English, and very dumb, and inside a few hours had begun an argument with the Canadian which went on, with intervals, all the afternoon. When Night Sister came on duty they were practically shouting at one another. She went to each in turn and told them to be quiet as they were disturbing the whole wing.

"Hen-toed, goose-rumped old harpy," said the young officer when she had gone out, looking about the ward for encouragement. Martin put down his paper.

"You!"

"Yes, sir."

"Don't you ever make a crack like that again."

"I'm sorry, sir."

"You disgusting little twerp."

"I'm awfully sorry, sir, I had no idea. . . ."

"No idea that she's a fine woman and a good nurse!" He picked up his paper and rolled on to his side.

We grunted our agreement.

# Record Flight

# Record Flight

The flight was scheduled to start on a Monday but bad meteorological conditions in southern Europe and trouble with a petrol pump delayed us for several days. We lived at an hotel near the factory aerodrome and were objects of some interest to the other guests.

Jack drank steadily and said little, while Chuck, who had come up to see us off and was by far the most nervous of the party, played his guitar for hours on end and tried, without much success, to keep the conversation away from aviation. Moira was very much on edge, chain-smoking and rushing about in her car or cadging flights at the aerodrome. I went about with her, sometimes impatiently eager to start, but on other occasions conscious of a feeling of relief when it was finally decided that another day must be spent hanging about on the ground. I was dreaming whenever I slept, recurring ever-fearful dreams of crossed elevator controls, fire in the air, structural failure and crashing; the sky dark overhead.

One of the firms who were backing the flight was pressing us to risk the weather, as they wanted the advertisement of our success by the end of the week and their representative strolled about the tarmac all day and most of the night haranguing any of us he could find.

At last a knock at my door brought me swimming upwards out of a dream and Jack in shabby leather jerkin came in with a weather report in his hand.

"The weather's all right except for the odd storm. I think we should get off in an hour. You're all set, aren't you?"

"Yes, old boy, everything's on the top line. I'll be there in twenty minutes," I said, feeling cold in my guts. It was still dark and I shivered a little as I dressed, though the night was warm. In the distance a church clock was striking and I began to count the strokes, thinking as I used to at school: "If it's three it'll be all right, if it's three it'll be all right, if it's three I won't be flogged for Greek prose in the morning, if it's three it'll be all right. Oh God! Let it be three!"

Moira was already downstairs sipping hot coffee, warming her hands on the cup. I kissed her and we ate the sandwiches in silence. When we had finished the barman came in. He was an ex-artilleryman with a repertoire of improper stories extensive beyond his calling.

"Is there anything I can do, sir?"

"Thanks, no, Harry," Moira said. "It was sweet of you to get up for us."

"You're really going?" he asked.

"Yes," I said.

He felt in the pocket of his white jacket and produced a little Saint Christopher medal.

"Would Madam accept this with the best wishes of the Staff?"

"That's really a kind thought," Moira said. "Thank you so much." She read the inscription. "'*Regarde Saint Christophe, puis va t'en rassuré.*' Now this will certainly bring us luck."

We began to gather up our things.

"Good luck, sir, to you, and to you, Madam!"

Moira thanked him again and slipped her hand under my elbow as we went out.

"Thrilled, darling?"

"Yes," I said.

The small crowd standing on the apron before the hangars included a few newspaper men and flashlights leapt out of the darkness as we walked to the machine. We started the engines and then waited for them to warm up. I went for a walk across the aerodrome with Chuck. It was beginning to get light and soon birds were singing in a coppice on the western boundary.

"Hark at 'em," Chuck said, "singing like bastards this time in the morning. It might be a good thing to be a bird sometimes."

"With a little luck we'll be in India inside a day," I said.

"When I first came over here," Chuck went on, "I sure didn't like it."

"We've got de-icers, variable pitch airscrews, retractable undercart, plenty of speed, full blind-flying equipment, and all the navigational gubbins . . . it ought to be easy."

"Everything was so tidy and old looking. Then there was the way you'd find kids playing in the main drag and everyone drove on the wrong side of the street and there were shoe shops everywhere and the public lavatories were a disgrace."

"All there is to this business is to keep the fans turning."

"Then there's this social racket you find over here," Chuck continued, "that surely gets me down still. But I've grown to like the rest of it, especially in the south, where the trees meet over the roads. There's something restful about it too that kind of grows on you, if you get me . . . the funny little cottages with smoke curlin' up from the chimneys and pretty little country pubs where you play darts with the locals . . . and hay wagons pushing back the hedges as they go down the lanes."

"The navigation will be mostly D.R. In a way I'd have liked wireless, especially if we have to force-land somewhere in the wilds."

"Mind you," Chuck said, "I'm not crazy on this country. Gimme back home anytime. Maybe it's changed since I left, but it sure was grand when I was a kid going down to Belle View Park in the evenings in the fall and holdin' a girl's hand and watching the boats go by on the river."

If we break our necks on this trip, I thought, the silly things we're saying will be remembered and our foolish actions recalled by those who knew us. And they, seeking to justify death, pandering to a theatrical and illogical desire to ring down a perfect curtain on a poor production, will give import to our words, dignity to our actions, even finding reason in the whole undertaking.

We walked slowly back and listened to Jack running up the engines. Then everything was ready, more photographs were taken, everyone was shaking hands, someone gave Jack a horseshoe, I was kissed by a barmaid I'd known years before. Chuck squeezed into the cabin with us.

"Good luck, you kids, and happy landings . . . don't get bumped off . . . I don't like drinking on my own!"

Jack waved away the chocks, a mechanic put up his thumb and we started to taxi out accompanied by a ragged cheer and a waving of hats. I leaned over from the second pilot's seat and set the first course on the magnetic compass.

At the far end of the aerodrome Jack turned into wind, pumped on thirty degrees of flap, felt both airscrew controls to check that they were in fine, wound the tail incidence adjustment a quarter forward, tried the petrol cocks and magneto switches. Then he let off the brakes and pulling back the override levers opened both throttles.

Slowly we began to move and he brought the tail up. Half-way across we were bumping and then he brought her off and held her down to gain speed. Owing to the heavy load of petrol the *Marie Lou* climbed slowly. He pumped up his flaps and undercart, throttled down, changed both airscrews into coarse and turned slowly to bring us back over the aerodrome on our course.

I smiled at Moira, who was gripping my arm. Through my side window I could see the aerodrome, an untidy field below, the shabby hangars pushed up into one corner of the apron that shone with recent rain.

I had only time to take a back bearing and work out a wind before we were in the clouds. Jack continued to climb and at nine thousand feet we were in a hail storm. He reached down and turned the gyros on to pump drive so that when the A.S.I. dropped to zero there was no change in our rate of climb.

At twelve thousand we came suddenly into the sunshine, the white floor of cloud stretching for hundreds of miles before us. Jack levelled off, flying to an exact computed airspeed of two hundred and fifty-five. Each detail was so known to us, anything that had to be done so perfectly understood, every manœuvre and decision so often discussed and rehearsed, that we were like automatons, our feelings a hindrance to us.

I thought as I watched Jack how fitted he was to be a pilot. Rigorous training and experience had given him confidence tempered with perfect judgement. He was a machine as he sat by my side poker-faced, holding the *Marie Lou* on her course, his eyes sweeping the instruments every few seconds, and could be trusted to fly like a machine, to utilize his skill, undeterred by fear, and his judgement, unaffected by fatigue, to the utmost limit of human endurance.

We flew on for hour after hour, seeing nothing of the earth but the peaks of mountains standing up through the clouds, the only other moving thing our shadow which raced silently beneath us, following every curve of the clouds with effortless grace. Above was the dome of heaven, a nightmare blue except for the blazing ball of the sun, no trace of cloud to break its pitiless emptiness. The one sound in our ears was the roar of the engines mingling with airscrew thrash.

We were alone, racing through a dead world.

After six hours Moira took over, at first enthusiastic over the piloting but quickly becoming bored so that she needed constant watching to prevent her from wandering a few degrees off her course.

Then we went into another storm, the *Marie Lou* bumping about the sky, pitching and rolling while hail and snow came in through the edges of the windows. Jack took the controls again and Moira crouched at my side as I worked over the navigation. Jack, altering his height, was juggling with his throttles when the port motor began to bang. I leapt to his side and we watched supercharger pressure and revolutions. The trouble only occurred at twenty-two hundred and he pulled back the flap of his helmet and shouted, asking me what I made of it.

"Can't be plugs," I said; "must be automatic boost control piston sticking."

He thought for a few seconds then held up a thumb and turned his attention to piloting once more, the engine running normally as he opened the throttle. I offered Moira a chicken sandwich. She shook her head.

"Try it, my dear, it'll do you good."

"Don't feel like eating. . . ." she shouted.

"It's the effect of altitude . . . try it!" But she smiled and refused again. Already she seemed tired.

When we came out into the clear weather it was beginning to get warm and I changed with Jack, sitting in my shirt sleeves leaning my face against the window-edge to try and get the most of the cool wind that sang in the narrow opening. Moira had lost interest in the countries over which we were passing and lay on the floor trying to sleep. The starboard engine began to run hot, the oil temperature rising to ninety-five, and I had to throttle down, upsetting our scheduled average speed.

Hour after hour we sat there. Our clothes were wet with sweat, the wheel was sticky in my hands, and my sun-glasses slithered on the bridge of my nose. At one time it became very bumpy and Moira was sick. The oil pressure on the starboard engine had dropped a little and was worrying me. I told Jack that I'd have to inspect the pump when we landed.

"That'll shove our schedule back still further!"

"Can't be helped . . . we don't want the ruddy thing to pack up in the desert."

We found our first refuelling point easily, being dead on our track. The oil pressure had crept up again and I began to feel better.

"Would you like to take her in?"

"No . . . you carry on."

I throttled down, dropped the undercarriage,

changed the airscrews into fine, pumped on twenty degrees of flap, and put her down a little fast. A few officials greeted us and took Jack and Moira over to the aerodrome buildings for a rapid meal while I supervised refuelling and got the starboard covers off. I was a little deaf and my right leg hurt below the knee from the strain of holding on rudder. Handicapped by inadequate tools it took me some time to do my inspection. When I had finished Jack was standing by my side.

"I think it's all right," I said, "as far as I can see. What's the weather like?"

"The weather's grand."

"Where's Moira?"

"That's the trouble . . . she's been sick again and doesn't want to go on."

"I'll go and talk to her," I said, "just start up, will you?" In a sparsely furnished room in the airport buildings decorated with framed pictures from *The Tatler* I found her slumped into a wicker chair.

"Hullo, my dear," I said quietly, "d'you feel better now?"

"Yes."

I drank a cup of coffee and ate a sandwich.

"If you're all set . . . we'll get started."

"Oh, Paul . . . please don't think I haven't got the guts . . . but I can't go on . . . I just can't go on. You two go on and I'll follow you by Dominions."

"I know how you feel."

"It's being sick all the time. And there's no glamour in it . . . you just go on and on and on. I'm tired of it . . . tired of the inside of that aeroplane and the cramped conditions and the cabin full of petrol tanks and listening to the engines and the heat. I never thought it would be like this."

"It's rotten for you, I know," I said.

"And soon now it'll be dark . . . hours of it alone up there . . . if anything goes wrong we'll be . . . just broken up out there in the desert hundreds of miles from anywhere. When I used to watch you night flying at home . . . it was romantic . . . even that night you took me up it was an adventure . . . but now it's useless . . . just a jeopardizing of our future happiness for nothing. . . ."

"Come on, darling, you're in this, you and I and Jack, the three of us together."

"I thought that too, once. But what use am I? I can only keep the gyro on 'O'. I can't fly on a magnetic compass, navigate, take off or land, or even trim the *Marie Lou.*"

"Yes, my dear," I said softly, "but we're going now . . . Jack's got the motors going. Everyone feels like you do sometimes . . . you'll be fine again soon."

"That's the tragedy of it," she stared straight before her, twisting her hands back to back and interlocking her fingers. "You and Jack are just machines, but there must be many pilots broken by years of flying, by crashes, by war, who must feel as I do now . . . then they've got to earn bread by the only way they know and they dull themselves with drink and drive themselves into the sky with superhuman effort." She looked up at me. "In a few years what courage the aeroplane has taken out of the world!"

"Darling . . . it's time to go!"

Slowly she got to her feet and followed me across the sandy aerodrome to the sweltering cockpit of the *Marie Lou* in which we had still to speed over nearly half the earth.

Soon after we took off it grew dark and we flew beneath high cloud, seeing no light, navigating on dead reckoning. Jack decided to get some sleep and I did the piloting, singing and repeating verse to keep myself awake. Sometimes I became drowsy, trying to remember where we were heading, and would dream, though half awake, and think of Moira objectively as being hundreds of miles away in England, suddenly realizing with a start that she was crouching behind me.

The engines ran perfectly as it became colder but it was still bumpy and Moira was sick several times.

"When's it going to get light?" she asked.

"Soon, darling."

"It's awfully lonely."

"You'll feel better when dawn comes."

"Paul?"

"Yes?" I was straining to catch her words, for I was now fairly deaf.

"I'm glad I came on."

"Of course you are, darling," I said watching the starboard oil temperature, which was rising again.

"You don't despise me for not wanting to?"

"I admire you for admitting it."

"You were sweet the way you made me stick . . . I'm frightened now . . . but I'd have been much more frightened if it had got about that I'd lacked the guts to go on."

"That's the answer to a lot of bravery," I said.

After two hours or so Jack woke automatically, blaspheming lustily when he saw that I had throttled down. He asked how late I thought we should be at our next refuelling point.

"Working on dead reckoning . . . don't know the wind . . . about an hour!"

He nodded and glanced over his shoulder at the little flames swirling from the starboard exhaust, which were the only things to be seen from that window. My eyes were tired, my legs a little stiff. I wondered how I should feel on the following night.

Suddenly there was a terrific noise in the port engine. The boost needle shot up from minus one to zero, the revolution counter sagged out of sight as I slammed the throttle back, ramming on right rudder to hold the *Marie Lou* on her course.

"What the hell's the matter?" bawled Jack, his face red.

"The supercharger's blown up . . . the whole motor's gone," I said, opening the other engine up to maintain height.

"How long is it till daylight?"

"Just an hour."

"What about going back?"

"Better to go on, the river's only two hundred miles away." He shot a glance at the oil temperature, then looked at me and grinned.

"What's the least you can hold her up on?"

"She's doing 'em now."

I followed several obscene words on his lips. Moira, white-faced, pushed in between us, asking what was the matter.

"It's all right," Jack said, "we're flying on one motor to cool the other."

"You're skipper," I said, "would you like to take over?"

"I would, old boy."

We changed places. Now I had nothing to do but watch the wretched oil temperature and imagine that I could see signs of the dawn. We were losing height very gradually and I could feel Moira trembling through her thin frock as she leaned against me.

"Darling?" she spoke so that Jack was out of earshot, "is it really dangerous?"

"No, there's nothing to worry about," I said. I was thinking how we had both lied to her, wondering at this childish subterfuge employed by the strong towards those they imagine weaker than themselves, in that far from serving to lull fear it adds dread to doubt, tempers wonder with vague fear.

Just after it was light on the ground the starboard engine burst an oil pipe, the brown liquid covering the underneath of the wing and coating my navigation window. Now we had to come down. We were flying at six thousand feet and all around was the desert, brown and empty for hundreds of miles. The silence as we glided fell strangely on our ears and we strained our eyes to distinguish the surface below.

Jack dropped his wheels, turned off his petrol cocks and sat there expressionless, his rugged face, its purposeful features enhanced by crash scars, clear against the early light.

Soon we saw that the ground was level and almost covered with large boulders throwing purple shadows. Jack picked what seemed to be a clear patch and, watching it over his shoulder, went into a gentle turn pumping on as much flap as he wanted, just as if he was coming in to land at an aerodrome. I smiled to see him, from pure habit, glance about the sky for signs of other aircraft as he turned into a straight glide.

Now we were skimming boulders, seeming to

be travelling so slowly that an impact would be of little consequence, a thought hardly endorsed by the ninety miles an hour that showed on the A.S.I. Then Jack put twenty pounds on the brakes and the *Marie Lou* went down for a good landing.

In the dead silence I thought I could hear the gyros still running, but it may have been imagination, for my ears still rang with the roar of the engines. Jack took his hands off the wheel and wiped the sweat off his face with his sleeve.

"That's the end of the record," he said.

The record, I thought. Of course, that's the end of the record.

We climbed out and stood in the shade of the fuselage, for it was already warm. After some seconds Moira asked where we were.

"About a hundred miles from a Royal Air Force Station," I said.

"Will they search for us?"

"As soon as they know we're missing and what track we were on."

"How long will that take?"

"They'll be on the job this evening," I said.

"Do you think they'll find us?"

"Oh, yes. They use a scientific method of search."

"Then there's nothing to do but wait?"

"That's all, my dear."

Jack produced a small bag from the rear of the fuselage. It contained ground strips, which we proceeded to lay out, surgical dressings, and iron rations. The latter, together with what we had in the cockpit, would last us for about three days, while the liquid at our disposal could be eked out for a similar period. Jack suggested that I helped him to gather dried-up scrub to form a heap for firing should we sight an aircraft.

"D'you think they'll find us?" I asked when Moira could no longer hear.

"Not a hope. I was out here years ago flying nine acks. I know this country well."

"That's cheerful!"

"Cheerful's the word."

Later I took the starboard covers off and did a thorough inspection. Jack watched me, saying nothing. The heat now was intense and I was plagued by flies. Moira slept uneasily under the fuselage. Now and again I fancied I could hear aircraft, but the only objects in the sky were a species of vulture strange to me. About midday I lay down for a rest, taking a half-cigarette that my companion offered.

"D'you think she'll go?" he asked.

"I'll get the starboard going," I said, "but the port's mucked to blazes."

He lit a match and watched it without lighting his cigarette till it burnt his fingers. "The test pilot told me she'd take off on one motor," he said. "If we clear a few rocks away down to the south there, there'll be plenty of run."

"It's taking the hell of a chance," I said.

"Do you remember those blokes in Australia?"

"Yes."

"After they'd drunk the alcohol out of the compass they walked round the kite till they died."

"I remember," I said.

"There's *her* to think of."

"I'm willing to try."

"We'll settle that later. How soon d'you think you can get her going?"

"Not before dusk. But we've two flashlamps and with luck she'll be ready by dawn to-morrow. I'll have to rob the port engine, that'll take the time."

"Right . . . I wish I could do more to help."

"You've done plenty already," I said, "leave this to me; it'll soon be finished."

. . . . .

But things went wrong. First my tools left much to be desired, as a full fitter's kit would have been too heavy to carry. Then in order to reach parts of the engines I had to stand on Jack's shoulders. Towards evening I began to feel giddy from working long hours in the sun, and once I fell, bringing Jack down with me and bruising my shoulder.

At last it grew dark and as the work was too intricate to be done by flashlamp, I gave up for the day and had my first meal lying by Moira's side. It was a lovely night, the sky filled with stars.

"I feel responsible for all this," she said suddenly.

"For all what?" I asked.

"This being out here," she said.

"Nonsense," Jack put in.

"But I do . . . I was the tough one . . . I was the one who always wanted to go." She laughed quietly and bitterly. "Why, Paul even tried to stop me once and now I lie here all day and watch him working in the sun. You see I had the wrong idea of it. . . . I thought a lot about the crowds at the other end and used to rehearse little speeches to them . . . but I never thought of being out here . . . just sitting in the desert waiting for someone to rescue us."

"In three months time", Jack said, "you'll be starting out again, probably on this same run. This game gets into your system." He thought for a few seconds. "On my last trip I got smashed up. When I promised Eve I'd give it up and live a normal sort of life I really meant it. But it wasn't long before I was itching to be off again."

No-one spoke for some time and when it grew colder we got into the cabin and I lay awake with a splitting headache listening to the regular breathing of my companions, my mind filled with the technicalities of aero engine oil systems.

The next morning was worse, I fell twice before midday and Jack was beginning to feel the strain of holding me. The second time I hit my head and regained consciousness in Moira's lap. Then I had a meal of iron rations and went to work again. My head was swimming and I had to keep one arm round a blade of the airscrew to keep myself upright on Jack's shoulders. The flies seemed worse, and forgetting Moira's presence I began to curse and blaspheme till Jack twitched my trouser leg.

"I'm sorry, Moira . . . it's this pump housing."

"That's all right," she answered.

I had lost all sense of time, the only thing in my

mind being the determination to get the engine running with full oil pressure.

At last it was done and it only remained to transfer the oil from port to starboard engine. For this we used a thermos flask and I grew unspeakably weary, counting each trip and saying "ten more", "ten more", "ten more", "do ten more", till the engine was full. Then I tried to start up, but for some reason the engine was obstinate, refusing to catch, and soon she was rich and I had to wait. This went on until the battery ran out.

"What now?" Moira asked.

"One of us will have to stand on the other's shoulders again and turn her over with the handle," I said.

"Not to-night," Jack said, "it's too late now."

So we walked out into the desert and began to roll away boulders, clearing a runway. Moira's hands were soon bleeding and I was dazed, imagining that Chuck was with us. Finally we reached two large rocks, firmly embedded.

"That's all we can do," Jack said.

"It isn't very long," Moira said.

"It's long enough," the other answered.

We went back and lay in the shade of the aircraft. The food and drink were nearly finished and Jack put us on half rations. Moira had been asking all day when the Royal Air Force were going to find us, but now she was silent, realizing how slender the chances were. Jack was quiet too, walking slowly round the *Marie Lou.*

"Paul, darling, you look terribly ill!"

"I'm fine," I said. "How d'you feel?"

"I'm fine, too."

"Does your head hurt?"

"No," I said.

She put a damp bandage across my forehead. "Is that better?"

"That's grand," I said, "but you're wasting water."

"Do you remember the first time we met?"

"I remember."

"Regrets?"

"No regrets."

"Whatever happens?"

"Whatever happens," I said.

"At first I thought you only wanted to seduce me!"

"Didn't I?"

"Darling, I love being seduced by you."

"You're going to marry me, as soon as——"

"We get out of this."

I rolled on to my bad shoulder, the pain stabbing my consciousness so that I quickly rolled back again.

"We don't know each other very well, do we?" I said.

"What do you mean?"

"You never fool me when you're pretending to be dull."

"This game we play of keeping up our spirits and hoping?"

"We don't have to. We'll get out of this if we have to walk it."

"Now you're playing it."

"I'm sure we'll get out," I said. "I'm just a bit browned off now and then, that's all."

I slept a little that night, dreaming that I was in England in the autumn, the apples red on the tree in the Rectory garden at home and my people alive and the smell of leaves burning and horse chestnuts dropping on the lawn and the sky very blue and my father walking over from church after changing the colours, his thumb holding his spectacles on the cover of a black leather Bible.

When I awoke I felt better and after some rancid coffee I primed the carburettors and started to turn the heavy engine over, Moira sitting at the controls. Suddenly she kicked and started. Dead beat I nearly fell into the airscrew as I pulled the handle out, but Jack bent his knees and pulled me clear.

As soon as she was warm I tested her to full revolutions, the *Marie Lou* straining at the stones we used as chocks. Then I throttled down again and switched off.

"Pressure's O.K.," I said. "She's fine."

"Grand!" Jack said, "but what did you cut the switch for?"

"We've forgotten to jettison the long-range tank!"

"Hell! I never thought of it . . . let it go now . . . it'll soon evaporate in this heat." I turned the cock as he spoke and hundreds of gallons of petrol poured out into the desert, washing about the wheels. Some time later when we judged the risk of fire from a flash to be negligible, I climbed on Jack's shoulders for the last time and started up once more.

Again I got into the pilot's seat and tried her up to full revolutions.

"You did a good job there," Jack said. "Just

hop out of that seat and I'll be in civilization in an hour."

"Don't talk tripe," I said. "You stay here with Moira while I have a stab at it. I weigh less than you and she'll be off the deck sooner."

"I'm skipper," Jack said, "and I'm going."

"Toss you for it!" I said. My voice sounded very far away.

"You two have got each other," Jack said. "I've only my job left and this is part of it."

"I've got the navigation buttoned," I said.

"Navigation my foot," Jack answered. "I can smell my way in from here."

"I think Jack ought to go," Moira said. "You're not very well, you know, darling."

"All right," I said. Without warning I felt very weary. "Now this is our approximate position marked here," I showed him the map. "Fly on this course, I'm allowing you four degrees for drift, and you'll be dead on your track when you hit the river. At midday Moira and I will have a ruddy great fire going . . . they can't miss us."

"I'll lead 'em in," Jack said.

I felt awkward.

"Good luck," Moira said and kissed him. Her eyes were filled with tears.

"Good luck, you old monkey," I said, "take it easy if she doesn't seem to be coming off."

He nodded and I touched his shoulder and followed Moira out of the cabin. Then I levered the stones from before the wheels and held up my thumb. He flashed a grin through a healthy growth of beard, pumped on flap, opened the engine till the aircraft began to strain. Then he let off the brakes and the *Marie Lou* began to move.

Slowly, so slowly the machine moved down the runway and I stood my hand on Moira's arm, urging speed, more speed, with all my strength, trying with useless effort of mind to force the *Marie Lou* into the air. It took Jack hundreds of yards to get the tail up and I could see by the elevators that he was making desperate attempts to bounce the aircraft off.

"He'll never do it!" Unconsciously I spoke aloud. "Maybe we didn't jettison enough juice."

Moira's mouth was twisted with anguish. I was looking almost up sun, which hurt my eyes. The machine still showed no signs of becoming airborne. "Throttle back, you fool!" I shouted. As he travelled faster he found it difficult to hold her straight. My companion gave a little cry and turned her face into my shoulder.

The *Marie Lou* hit a large boulder with her starboard motor, swirling into a cloud of dust out of which the port wing tip could be seen as a rock tip standing out of the sea.

In a few seconds the roar of the crash, the crackling and splintering, the anguish of intricate machinery rent asunder, broke upon us, then rumbled away over the desert, leaving horrible silence and a cloud of settling dust and the vultures wheeling and swaying on their broad wings overhead.

I began to run.

•

As I ran I thought I was at school again, doubling round the big field before early school, a little sick with running on an empty stomach, my breath rasping in my throat, wondering how far behind the whipper-in was, dreading the inevitable blow with a buckled belt if I should lag, my mind busy with the day's work, hoping I could keep out of trouble with my Greek syntax for another day.

It seemed that as I ran the wreckage was receding and I wondered, as I had done several times in the past few hours, if I was going mad, or whether the whole affair was but a nightmare and I should wake, perspiring, into the grey tranquillity of an English dawn and, hearing the singing of the birds, be happy to be alive and well.

I was above all conscious of a great loneliness, feeling that an audience, shocked with interest, would have comforted me, and in some small way have compensated for the tragedy.

Then I saw the first of the flames and stopped in my tracks, the sweat gathering in my eyebrows, hopeless fear welling in my guts. Moira caught me up. Her hair hung over her face, she gulped her breath, leaning forward and holding her side. One of her high heels was missing. She was oil-stained.

The fire grew in intensity, sending a great cloud of smoke over the sunburnt landscape, and as we approached we could hear the crackling, feel the heat brushing our faces.

I stopped and held her arm.

"It's no good," I said.

"Isn't there anything . . . we can . . . do?"

"Nothing," I said.

"Is he . . . alive . . . in there?"

"No," I said.

"You needn't lie now, darling." Her voice was quiet.

"I'm not lying, my dear. He must have been dead before the fire started."

"Why?"

"You could hear him scream from here," I said.

"I hadn't thought of that."

She suddenly began to cry.

"Paul, darling! What's going to happen to us? What's going to happen to us? I'm terrified!"

I started to reassure her, marvelling that the stupid stock phrases I uttered, the inarticulate illogical arguments I cited, could, as indeed they did, soothe her so that presently she sobbed softly in my arms.

It was Moira who first saw him.

He limped out of the smoke on the leeward side, bleeding from a cut on his cheek, his left arm swinging loosely, his flying-jacket cut to ribbons.

We stood speechless as he came towards us. Then my companion rushed up and caught his arm. He smiled at us.

"So they take off on one engine!" he said. "Wait till I see that bloody test pilot."

• • • • •

He put his arm on my shoulder and we walked to the far end of the runway, where we had left the first-aid kit.

"She didn't seem to be coming off!" I said.

"I couldn't do anything with her, though she was gaining speed all the time."

"How did you get out?" Moira asked.

"Got a bang on the head . . . when I came round I could feel the heat . . . I wriggled through the window as quick as I damn well could."

Moira did what she could with iodine and bandages, then left us for a while. Jack was very white.

"I don't like it," he said.

"Have you broken your arm?"

"Don't know . . . quite probable."

I divided a cigarette.

"We're up the creek this time."

"And no paddle."

He puffed his half till it glowed. When he spoke again his voice was slow with thought.

"I've seen a lot of blokes buy it, but I never thought much about dying . . . not till now, that is." He felt his shoulder tenderly. "D'you think it helps to be religious or anything?"

"I don't know," I said.

"Some of those religious types shoot a pretty

line about it . . . but they seem just as much afraid as anyone else . . . in any case they're worrying about what happens afterwards. I don't care about that . . . I'll take a chance on anything. It's sitting here on my arse waiting for a sticky end that doesn't appeal to me."

"I feel that way, too," I said.

He brushed cigarette ash from his sleeve absently.

"If there's another world and they don't fly," he continued, "I don't want to go there. And if they do . . . well . . . I've done an awfully long time in cockpits already."

"We took a chance," I said.

"And had bad luck."

"No, old boy, it's not a question of luck . . . if you take a chance you must be prepared for this . . . otherwise it wouldn't be a chance."

"Perhaps you're right . . . but just let me get out of this and luck or no luck, chance or no chance . . . I'll break this mucking record if it takes me the rest of my life."

We made a pathetic little tent out of the ground strips to keep off the sun. I grew delirious again, imagining that Chuck was coming to rescue us.

The next thing I knew I was in Moira's arms.

"Better, darling?" she rocked my head in her lap.

"Yes," I said. "How long have I been out?"

"Not long."

"If only we could *do* something?"

"I know, Paul," she said. "I know."

How we dramatize our lives, I thought, imagine we are secretly superior to our fellows, conjecture ourselves as masters of intricate situations, live, in our minds, gargantuan existences that can never be endorsed by the world. Even in this scene I felt, not so much despair at our predicament, as a sense of frustration, a lack of colour, an intense annoyance at the idea of a slow death in the depths of the desert, exciting only the professional interest of the vultures.

"Don't worry, darling," she went on. "Jack says they'll see the smoke as they search and so find us. It's going to be all right, really darling, it's going to be all right." I made no reply and she continued: "Jack's been in tougher spots than this and so have you . . . there's really nothing to bother about. All we have to do is to wait."

"When there was work to be done," I said, "it was I who comforted you. Now you've turned the tables on me and it's you who have the patience and the courage."

She smiled, pushing her fingers in my hair.

"We seem to be the two halves that Plato spoke of . . . was it Plato?"

"I'm afraid I don't remember," she said.

"It doesn't matter, now, anyway."

"Darling?"

"Yes," I said.

"You remember how, when I first took over the controls of the *Marie Lou*, I got tired so quickly?"

"Yes."

"You were annoyed?"

"No."

"Why were you annoyed?"

"I wasn't annoyed."

"Because I was overcorrecting and because I really couldn't cope . . . because I was just a hindrance?"

"I was thinking of you as a man——"

"As a pilot?"

"If you like."

"I knew . . . I was afraid . . . it seems stupid . . . I was afraid you wouldn't love me any more!"

I caught her hand and kissed it.

"That's over now."

"I'm glad," she said, "especially about the love part."

"When I say that's all that's left to me," I answered, "I'm not using a line out of a jazz song."

I grew drowsy and the voices of the others became senseless, losing all animation, and binding, thatched my mind so that I slept once more, pain forgotten in the merciful kin of death.

Then I saw Jack and Moira waving frantically and firing pyrotechnics while a Service aircraft circled overhead. God! I thought, another dream. For how many days now had I been seeing machines? Hearing fighters? The scream of the blower mingling with the wind in the wires, with airscrew noise and the engine's song? Or twins coming in to land with the motors popping as the airscrews overran the throttle settings? Or light aeroplanes with the purr of their tiny hundred-horse-power engines?

This was worse in its actuality, for I recognized the type, a Royal Air Force Moose fitted for desert flying, saw the pilot looking over his shoulder as he approached, noticed details of fuselage and empennage, heard the rumble as she went down for a three-point landing.

Then Moira came limping towards me, wringing her hands and laughing hysterically and I knew that it was no dream.

"You were lucky," the pilot said as we ate the supplies he had brought. "I'd finished my search detail and was going back to the aerodrome when my gunner saw your red light."

"We thought you'd missed us," Jack said.

"We had to find you." The pilot was young and blue-eyed, shy and tremendously pleased at having located us. "I got a bearing from base on the long aerial before we landed. The lads will be here in a brace of shakes."

"What an awful country this must be to fly in," Moira looked up from a chicken sandwich.

"It's not bad actually, Miss Barratt. We get plenty of hours in and there's usually active service round the corner. Some sheik or other is always starting trouble, and believe you me, his troops are no cissies. Then we buy Arab ponies in the villages, break 'em ourselves and get some polo, which is pretty wizard on a Flying Officer's pay...."

There was something I wanted to ask him, I struggled to remember what it was, hearing a great roaring, conscious of a splitting headache. Then my knees wobbled and I fell, uninterested in the flight hurrying to our rescue which would soon appear as specks on the horizon.

I was in hospital for some time and it was autumn when the boat train carried us up to Waterloo through the blue mists of a perfect English evening.

"What are you thinking about?" Moira asked softly.

I was gazing at the little villages sliding by, thatched and tree-bound in settled peacefulness. It seemed that in this scene there was not only a joyful sense of homecoming, but also an answer to all the striving in my nature. I thought of how, as a child, there was this sudden magic in ordinary things, this wonder in a known scene; how for no reason a flood of experience, almost indefinable, widened the narrow path of one's life.

"What are you thinking about?" she repeated.

"I was thinking about us," I said.

"How we'll always be in love?"

"Yes."

"Even when we're old?"

"Even when we're old."

Sitting beside me, her body warm by mine, her very youthfulness seemed to mock the content of her hackneyed words.

"And find happiness?"

"That too, my dear."

The sky behind the sheds was grey with dawn when we arrived and the metallic beginning of another day fell unkindly on the faces of the newspaper men, airport officials, photographers, and friends who were grouped about the monoplane, showing the strain in their tired faces. The wind that swept the aerodrome was cold so that Moira shuddered as she leaned against me and the electric lights in the offices appeared homely and unspeakably comforting.

"Where's Jack?" Moira asked.

"He'll be along right now." As Chuck spoke I saw his fellow pilot leave the control tower and walk towards us across the tarmac, a swashbuckler, in sheepskin-lined flying-coat (for it was winter, the country pitiless with streaks of dirty snow). Flashlights splashed in the darkness as he approached with microphone swinging beneath his chin and a little fat man and two girls running at his side.

"Remember, darling?"

"I remember," I said.

"It was good of you to come down," Jack began.

"I feel responsible, dragging staid married people out of bed at this hour."

"All set?" Chuck asked.

"Yes, the weather's good. We'll be off as soon as the engines are warm."

"Be careful, my dears," Moira said and then added pensively: "Now, I rather wish we were both coming with you!"

"You two don't want a record to make you happy."

We shook hands and Moira kissed them.

"All the luck in the world," I said. They smiled as they turned.

The roar of each motor cloaked all sound on the aerodrome, then Jack throttled down, waved away the chocks and taxied out, the noise now drowning the thin cries of the onlookers. The machine, heavy with petrol, rocked as it moved, seemingly ugly on the bristling legs of its undercarriage. But when it became airborne and the slowly rotating wheels tucked themselves into its belly, it turned into a silhouette of beauty, a slim and lovely thing tearing into the loneliness of the sunrise.

We stood arm in arm till the machine disappeared and the drone of its engines no longer fell upon our ears.

# Return to Life

# Return to Life

They had cut away my clothing at the hospital, so I borrowed flying-suit, helmet, and goggles from the locker-room and went out on to the aerodrome. It was a still, warm October day and the intimacy of my surroundings came back to me, the dim clatter of tools echoing through the hangars, the sweet smell of dope, the dust and little bits of grass swirling across the concrete apron as engines were run up, the slow flapping of the wind stocking at the corner of the watch office; these things enveloped my consciousness so that the previous weeks were forgotten and I might never have been away.

"D'you feel all right about it?" asked the Chief Instructor.

"I feel fine," I said, running the slip-knot of my scarf taut against my throat.

"There's nothing to worry about," he went on.

"I'm not worrying," I said.

"There were marks of her heels on the cockpit floor and the under side of the rudder—with the controls jammed like that no one could have got a 'plane out of a spin."

I nodded, jerked the zip-fastener tabs so that the clumsy flying-suit pulled itself about me, and went out to the aircraft.

"I'll take her round first," he said when I'd plugged the telephone lead home. I grunted, pulling on my harness straps, setting altimeter, petrol cocks and master switches. I did these things unthinkingly, the memory of the crash, revived by the familiarity of my surroundings, hooding my mind.

He taxied out, turned into the wind and took off. As the machine rocked across the aerodrome and then, becoming air-borne, soared smoothly upwards, I found myself following his movements, instinctively checking the synchronizing of bank and rudder as he pulled up into a climbing turn. But the intrinsic understanding of it had gone; I was a passenger, I no longer flew in my own mind.

At six hundred feet he turned again, levelling off, and I looked over the side, remembering the strangeness of the country when first I came to the flying club. How it had gradually etched itself into my mind, the essential shape of it, the pattern of wood and lake, the clear line of canal and railway. And how the time had come when I could dive out of the clouds during instrument flying instruction and, glancing at the ground, tell my pupil to fly on a certain bearing, knowing that, eventually, the untidy aerodrome would come sliding under a wing.

Now there was a light mist on the countryside, light mist on the woods that were touched with winter, on farm and village, stubble and tall trees with their delicate shadows rotting into the quiet fields, on ploughman and turnip-cutter, a light mist as the bloom on a plum that made one rub one's goggles with the back of one's glove.

The Chief Instructor turned once more, and throttling back, glided across wind. Then sideslipping in, landed on the circle.

"Will you take her round?" His voice was casual; too casual, I thought. As I pushed the throttle open I felt my hands and feet harden on the controls. The Chief, wise in twenty years of instruction, sensed it instantly, and as I wrenched the aircraft into the air I saw him look up sharply into the mirror that was mounted on the port centre section strut to enable an instructor to watch his pupil's face.

He began to whistle softly and placed his hands on the sides of the cockpit, as one does to give pupils confidence in themselves. I climbed up steadily until we reached three thousand feet.

"Try a spin, will you?"

Now I hated the casual note in his voice. I was rattled. He knew I was rattled. I turned and glanced downwards. There were no machines about. The haze had thinned with altitude and belonged to the ground. As I looked below I could see only the slabs of lake and pond and the hard lines of the railways glinting in the sunshine.

My hand was shaking as I throttled the engine down. I blasphemed softly, pulled the stick into my stomach, kicked on full rudder. The aircraft lurched into a spin, the horizon heeling upwards. Fear leapt inside me; it might have been my first flight. I set my teeth, hardening my mind against terror, trying to blot out the image of that last spin, my pupil frozen on to the controls, screaming and shouting while I fought to bring the machine out, laughing into the telephones in an effort to ride down her fear.

And now I thought of the ground, losing that map-like appearance imparted by height, twisting upwards and no fear any more but a great interest, observing every detail, thinking again and again: "It's happened to me—it's happened to me—I'm going to spin in——"

Then cutting the switches and pulling the petrol cock shut as we hit.

After that the silence and the smell of petrol and the pain in arm and side as I dragged my pupil clear, the pain making me feel sick, thickening the mist of panic that already threatened to cloud my mind.

And, when I realized that she was dead, the walk to the farm, awed by the silence, seeing nothing moving, no animal or living thing, hearing nothing, wondering if I were dead and this was the terrible loneliness of life after death. Then hope flooding my consciousness as I saw a child moving in the stinking farmyard.

I thought of how I groaned in spirit as I came along the stone walk to the back door, knowing how difficult it would be to make them realize the outline of my story, dreading the re-telling of each detail, trying all the while to build the fabric of my experience in my brain.

They *were* stupid, too, I crying inside myself for patience, thinking again and again: "Only a little while now—only a little while now"—speaking slowly, fighting the great fatigue that weighed down my understanding. The pain all this time crusting my body and the sweet taste of blood for ever in my mouth.

When the telephoning was done and I'd told the story for the last time that day, when the sightseers had rushed away to find the wreckage and there was no more noise, they took me to hospital, swinging on an ambulance stretcher, listening to the rattle of the engine (it wanted decarbonizing) and the water splashing in the tank above the iron-framed washbasin.

As we spun downwards two months later, the tart autumn air sighing in the bracing wires, I could still feel the pain of broken ribs and arm, of dislocated shoulder and crushed hand. I could still hear the flapping of the canvas curtain behind the driver and the driver's voice as he talked to his mate about a dart match he'd played the night before, breaking into long-drawn tactical explanations to ask again and again, "Are you all right, sir?" until his flaccid voice was inlaid in my consciousness.

When I had brought the Moth out of the spin the Chief Instructor asked me to take her back to the aerodrome and land. I flew badly, skidding on my turns, gliding now too fast, now too slow, my landings wretched, so that I could feel the Chief's hand on the dual control, guiding me. I was frozen on to the control column. After three circuits I began to find difficulty in getting into the aerodrome. He landed her himself.

"What's the trouble?" he asked, leisurely. We were taxi-ing in, and he swung his head from side to side of the cockpit, watching the flying-field on both sides of the engine.

"I don't know," I said. "I suppose that pile-up shook me a bit."

"Nonsense—a show like that does one good. Besides, you've crashed before, haven't you?"

"Yes," I said, "I've crashed before."

"Well, I want you to take her up yourself—fly round a bit and then try some landings. If they get too bad, come in."

"Right," I said, watching him getting out of the front cockpit. I felt for the hundredth time the strangeness of seeing someone physically remote climbing out of a cockpit after hearing his voice in one's ears in the clear emptiness of the sky, after checking the movements of his hands and feet on the dual control.

I went up and tried to fly. I was scared stiff, rigid on the controls. My movements were jerky; I was constantly over-correcting, glancing nervously from instrument to instrument. Flying level at two thousand feet, I thought of the hundreds of hours I'd flown subconsciously; how I'd cursed and sworn at pupils because they, petrified with fear, couldn't do what I was trying to do now.

I'd been up for perhaps ten minutes when I suddenly felt that I couldn't land. I thought of the words of an Air Force doctor in the days when I was training in the Service. He was white-haired and quiet, having been much with death, and he told us that every pilot is liable to reach a breaking-point, a time when his flying days are done. We laughed, I remember, being confident with the untried, arrogant confidence of youth.

It seemed that for me, this time had come. That I was finished, destined to crawl about the earth for the remainder of my life.

No more the feel of the engine roaring into life under one's hand, the joy of aerobatics when the horizon dipped and rolled and stick and rudder moved easily, firmly, quickly about the cockpit.

No more the rugged comradeship of flying men, but my part to live in the past, glorifying incidents I ought to be surpassing, repeating anecdotes that would become woven into the fabric of my life so that it wasted away till my living was merely a frame for my memories.

No more the pub-crawling; drinking in the happy atmosphere of village bars with flying folk till the world seemed a merry place. No more the aerobatics last thing at night, when the gallery of loungers and gin-sipping women at the club-house and the influence of the evening's alcohol brought one too near the ground, the fear of death glowing in one's mind.

I approached the aerodrome. A little group stood on the tarmac. Some of them were men and women I'd taught to fly.

I began to fray my body with my mind. "Land," I said. "Land, blast you!" The first attempt was a failure. I bounced high, put my engine on, fearing for the undercarriage, and went round the aerodrome again. I flew at two hundred feet, so as to leave less time to think as I came in. I turned very gingerly the last time and throttled down to glide. I could feel the sweat cold around my eyes, warm inside my gloves, gathering my shirt about my body. Now! I thought, and brought the stick back . . . back. . . back . . . watching the ground ahead as I'd never watched it since my first solo. When I thought the wheels were two feet above the ground I pulled the tail down, and with body tense and forearm rigid waited for her to stall. I felt the almost imperceptible shudder as she lost flying speed, and then she went down smoothly, softly, a perfect landing with the tail-skid rumbling on the sheep-cropped grass.

I twisted my head sharply to see if there was anyone coming in to land, and then took off again. I felt fine; bugles sang in my mind. I could land, flying was my job again, the future unruffled. I shouldn't have to look for work, for some mundane pen-pushing occupation. I climbed at the stall, rocking the stick to find out when the ailerons should lose control. At two thousand feet I slow-rolled, suddenly loving that feeling of hanging from the shoulder straps as you keep the stick forward to make her climb. Then I spun, stall-turned and half-rolled off a loop, bending my head back to watch the horizon come over. My hands were as smooth as silk. I went in, tail-swishing to drop the 'plane on the concrete apron before the hangars. The Chief Instructor came out. He was smiling, his helmet, which hung from his shoulders by the telephones, swinging as he walked. I could see the red mark beneath his chin left by the strip.

"All right?" he asked.

I grinned.

"All right," I said.

# Test Flight

# Test Flight

As the test-pilot walked out on to the tarmac he saw that the mechanics had already started the engine with a gas-starter, which two boys were wheeling away on a small trolley. It was difficult walking with a nineteen-pound Irvin parachute hanging behind one's knees, with fur-lined fug boots and a fleece-and-leather flying-suit that was confoundedly stuffy on a sultry June day. What wind there was flapped the wind-sock about the pole, blew up dust in little spirals from the bare patches where the 'planes were wheeled from the hangars and fluttered the writing-pads that were strapped above his knees.

Waiting for the mechanic, who had run up the engine to climb up the step-ladder, he drew on first his dirty silk gloves, then his leather gauntlets, and stooping, pulled in turn each of the parachute straps that hung clinking from the pack hard against the inside of each thigh and clipped them to their appropriate rings on the harness. The metal middle-wing monoplane rocked gently to the rhythm of her engine so that the sun danced in a thousand ever-changing places on her stubby fuselage. She was a new single-seat fighter with flaps, retractable undercarriage and a variable-pitch propeller. On the drawing-board she had been so vastly superior in design, in speed and performance to any fighter in the Service that the chief designer's task in persuading the directors to build her, in the hope of the Government adopting her for general use in the Air Force, had been an easy one. Now, as they stood in a silent, uneasy group in the board-room window, fat, stupid-faced men who were more at home in a golf-club bar, now that the 'plane was completed, they were not so certain.

To be sure, the Government were interested. (An official stood with them. An old pilot, lean and tall with hard blue eyes, wrinkled about by twenty years' flying, and fine square-fingered hands, who listened politely to all they had to say, smiled courteously at their jests, but said little.) But, they thought, Government interest did not justify the spending of £16,000. (Wind-tunnel tests on a model had necessitated expensive last-minute alterations.)

Before one of the hangars stood the score or so picked workmen who had been working on the 'plane for the previous eighteen months behind locked doors. They had watched her grow from finely-drawn plans, from four steel longerons (as the main members of an aircraft are called), with skilled, costly workmanship into the thing of beauty, streamlined to the last rivet-head, that was now to "go up on first test". So slowly had she evolved that it seemed to them she was part of the hangar that had seen her birth. A hangar now open to the aerodrome, containing now only tools, packing-cases, trestles, deserted work-benches, oil drums and dozens of rolled-up plans, all numbered and done up with coloured ribbons.

And each workman thought of the part he had played, down to the junior who had helped to blow up the tyres, the common pride of workmanship binding them into a comradeship that was above wage disputes, beyond discipline, untouched by personal feeling, so that when the junior, with the eager impetuosity of his age, asked the grim foreman standing next to him, "D'yer think she'll be O.K.?" he answered gravely as if speaking to an equal, "Eh, lad, I hope so . . . but tha' n'er can tell!" The test-pilot went slowly up the step-ladder, swung his legs into the cockpit, and sliding down, wriggled the pack of his parachute into the bucket seat. A mechanic who had clambered up after him helped with the straps of his aerobatic harness . . . left arm . . . right thigh . . . left thigh . . . right arm . . . he strained the narrow bands of webbing over the slotted pin on his chest and pushed home the locking web. As he thrust his toes into the rudder-bar straps, took the stick in his right hand and the throttle in his left, he glanced towards the roadway. He could see roofs of many cars above the hedge and a long white line of faces.

He felt for the pencils that were stuck into the top of his right fug boot, set the altimeter to zero and then, looking upwards (there was a good deal of broken cloud at four thousand) he touched first the magneto switches, then the petrol cock, then the locking web of his aerobatic harness, then the rip-cord ring of his parachute, memorizing their positions.

The cockpit was roughly fitted out, the incredible number of instruments, gun-sights, machine-gun synchronizing gear, bomb toggles, Sutton harness adjustment, flare-release and similar gadgets dear to Service experts were to be fitted later. He felt for the retractable undercarriage release handle and the manually-operated flap gear; both were in easy reach. Twisting his head he brought the stick hard back. Instantly three mechanics threw themselves on the tail. He began to open the throttle, watching the instruments. At fourteen hundred revolutions per minute he switched each magneto on and off in turn, the engine dropping between fifteen and twenty revs. And now he pushed the small steel lever fully forward and the eight hundred horse-power motor roared its pæan of power. Slipstream from the propeller beat down the grass in a wide circle, swept bits of loose paper and rag about the hangars, beat the mechanics' overalls fluttering about their bodies. The noise crashed in great waves of sound upon the minds of those near by. It was demoniac; so far unusual to the sightseers on the road that it brought with it a strange atmosphere of unreality, as in a dream in which the details are familiar but the outline horribly untrue. As they watched, a heavy lorry rumbled past unheard.

The test-pilot, subconsciously listening for any irregularity which might mean trouble, was outwardly unaware of the noise, watching his oil-pressure, his engine revs., his oil temperature. Satisfied, he throttled down again, the roar dying quickly to a rhythmic rattle.

Slowly, he waved his right hand from side to side. The two mechanics who had been waiting with the ropes in their hands jerked the wheel-chocks away, the port wing man saluting and pointing to a Gipsy Moth, belonging to the flying club who shared the aerodrome, which was coming in to land. As he turned down wind (turning on the ground was easy with wheel brakes) and instinctively eased the stick right forward so that the breeze blowing on the down-turned elevators would keep the tail down, he thought how good the mechanics were. But they were specially picked and subjected to long and arduous training. The average human being didn't take kindly to discipline and quick thinking

The monoplane picked her way fastidiously to the far end of the flying-field and as the pilot turned slowly into the wind his eyes once more searched the sky. But the Gipsy Moth had landed, bumping her way across the aerodrome and the sky was empty. He wound the tail-incidence forward, pulled down the old Meyrowitz goggles, rusted about the rims, that were suspended about his shabby helmet by two lengths of parachute-pack elastic, set the variable-pitch to "climb", held the stick hard back and pushed the throttle wide open. As she gathered speed he put the stick forward to bring the tail up, and then eased it back to central and waited for her to fly herself off. Just before the wheels lifted she swerved to port, hard opposite rudder hardly checking the yawing movement, so that she took off slightly out of the wind. He took a quick glance at the Air Speed Indicator, then pulled up in a steep climb, rocking the stick from side to side so that he should learn when the ailerons lost control and could therefore put the nose down some time before a wing would stall. Keeping an eye on the slots he pulled up the undercarriage and set himself to find the best climbing angle.

. . . . .

Ten minutes later he was flying level at nine thousand feet, and one of the writing-pads was covered with sprawling figures. He had found the stalling speed, the climbing and gliding angles, had flick-rolled and dived with throttle closed until the revs. screamed up from seven hundred to two thousand three hundred (the needle against the little red danger pointer, the earth, mist-ridden and unreal, swooping up to meet him, the stick hard in his hand as he stroked it back the sixteenth of an inch at a time).

"Now," he muttered, "a slow roll." He pulled the aircraft round in a tight circle, looking above and below. Then opening the throttle he pulled the nose above the horizon (the earth had no significance save as a checking medium) and put on full bank to the right, counteracting aileron drag by a touch of bottom rudder. He closed the throttle as he reached the vertical and, grunting as the 'plane went on to her back, pushed the stick forward to keep the nose up. He was now off the seat, hanging by the aerobatic harness. As he came up the other side the nose began to drop. He put on full right rudder, gave the engine a burst to get some slipstream on his tailplane, getting the stick back hard as the wing came up. But it was a dirty finish, the nose was down and forty degrees off the little cloud he had picked as a mark going in.

That must have looked rotten from the ground, he thought, glancing at each slot in turn to see if one were stuck open. But they were both closed. He was certainly impressing the Government bloke the wrong way; it was probably the rudder, the damn thing had looked too small anyhow. A spin would tell. He climbed to twelve thousand. One never knew what was going to happen in the first spin in a new type, especially when one was worried over the control in the yawing 'plane.

He flew level once more, made a note of the slow roll, looked below him and touched the rip-cord ring of his parachute. This sort of life was dangerous, there was no doubt of that. And yet, he reflected, closing the throttle and easing the nose up, that was how he liked it. When aviation became just another form of transport, when 'planes came to be universally fitted with compression-ignition engines, thereby eliminating the bogy of fire after a crash, when they could get down safely in any sort of field, when a simple and foolproof method of landing in a fog had been devised and every town had its airport . . . then he'd quit flying, and so would other pilots . . . who were flying now. He flew because it was risky, because it was exhilarating, because it called for the confidence that is born in the conquest of fear, for skill and coolness in danger.

The broken clouds were far below, white and hard, framing patches of the dim landscape that was studded with woods, laced by glittering bands of steel that he knew were railways, dappled by huge drifting pools of sunlight. He could just see the aerodrome with its regular boundaries, its marshalled hangars, its white landing-circle.

Queer to think he'd be having a drink down there in five minutes . . . if all went well. He was level with another layer of cloud, grey drifting cloud that hung in long drifting tendrils, obscuring the horizon. And now the airspeed had dropped to sixty-eight, the stick moved loosely in his hand. He kicked on full right rudder. Instantly the right wing went down. He pulled the stick right back. The nose dropped and the monoplane began to spin. The lower, whiter clouds came up to meet him, the horizon out of sight above, whirling about him. He watched the round shadow of his head flash over the instruments, counting the number of times he was turning. On the third turn the 'plane kicked and was forced into a spiral nose-dive by the slots. He went round once more and then put on top rudder and pushing the stick central (it had been forced to the right by autorotation) thrust it some six inches forward.

The monoplane spun as before. Fear rolled upwards in a great wave in his stomach.

"You bastard," he yelled and his voice was thin and ridiculous amidst the rushing wind. "Come out, God rot you!"

He rocked the stick full forward, kicking on full top rudder to no effect, the earth rolling upwards. He held the stick full forward and opposite rudder hard over, giving the engine burst after burst of full throttle, but it was of no avail.

He was very frightened, very cool, very certain of what he was going to do.

He pulled his feet from the rudder-straps, cut his magneto switches, pulled back the petrol cock, jerked the locking web out of the pin, thrusting his shoulders upwards so that the straps flew off.

It seemed that time had no reality, that he was living through an age of experience that could neither be measured by days nor years. The force of the spin threw him about the cockpit. He remembered being told that one had to get out on the inside as the centrifugal force of the spin would push one back if one attempted to climb over the outside. The clouds were very near now, he must have gone round at least nine times. If he didn't hurry he'd experience "black-out", which usually came after ten times round. ("Black-out" is the draining of the blood from the head by terrific centrifugal force, causing temporary blindness.)

He grabbed the cockpit side and stood on the seat with knees bent. Every action seemed to take an eternity, there was no contact with everyday living. To die, he thought, must be like this. Clutching his rip-cord ring he hurled himself head downwards over the side, feeling a sharp stab of pain as a wing-tip caught his leg a glancing blow, slitting the leather "fug" boot.

Now he was falling. It was terrible. He was so frightened that he found something akin to ecstasy in his fear, and above all a great familiarity as if he had been through all this before, had subconsciously known it was to happen, had lived his whole life for this one second. He waited till he should be well clear of the aircraft before cracking his 'chute. The spinning 'plane seemed to be shooting upwards. Vaguely he wondered if he would drift into its path.

He tore at the rip-cord, which came cleanly from its protective cable.

Thank God, the pins weren't bent. He'd never put on a 'chute again without looking at the pins which held the pack closed. Fool . . . the 'chute hasn't opened yet . . . something may go wrong . . . it may have been badly packed . . . I may fall into it . . . the shroud lines may be twisted.

Came a jerk that wrenched him into a sitting position. He swung gently in a great arc, looking upwards at a blessed white canopy that seemed to lean away as the clouds passed over it. As he passed through a hole in the clouds the monoplane shot by with the nose right down, spinning wildly. He watched it go down. It was hard to tell how high it was, aircraft a long way below one always seemed to be going into the deck. He hoped to hell it didn't fall on houses, on children, on the high road, anywhere where it would cause unhappiness . . . there was enough of that in the world. Would his switching off and closing the petrol-cock prevent fire? Probably not.

Perhaps he ought to have stayed in, tried some more to have got her out, people might say he was parachute-conscious and that wouldn't help a test-pilot. Besides there was a lot of money, work, ambition in that beautiful 'plane that no power on earth could now save from crashing into useless débris. The silence was new to him. Never in seven years' flying had he experienced anything like it. He could hear the soporific clatter of a train, the rattle of the fire-bell at the aerodrome and a tiny blob of sound that he knew was a motor-horn. It seemed he was hardly moving. Now surely the 'plane must crash. As the thought moulded itself in his mind he saw the monoplane crumple into the middle of a ploughed field, saw pieces of the cowling glint in the sun as they flew upwards. In a fraction of time it had lost its form and grace and become a blazing wreck, for as he watched, flames shot upwards and a tower of black smoke climbed lazily into the sky. In a few seconds he heard the roar of a crash and then there was silence again.

As he came near the ground he saw that the wind had risen since he had taken off. Just his luck. He would be dragged by the canopy. He didn't want to be dragged. Not with a leg that was dead below the knee.

The delusion that hew as suspended in mid-air had altogether disappeared, the ground came steadily upwards, drifting slowly by. The crowd who had lined the flying-field hedge were running up the road. Well, they were having their cheap thrill this time.

He landed heavily on his toes, falling forward,

his injured leg crumpling under him and was dragged nearly the whole length of the field before the canopy flapped into a lifeless carpet of silk.

He got uncertainly to his feet, stripped off his harness and gathered the canopy in his arms. The first of the sightseers approached, a thin, round-shouldered, spectacled man, his wan face flushed with the effort of running.

"Are you all right?" he panted, and his obvious anxiety robbed his words of their inherent absurdity. "Are you all right?" The pilot, who had been arranging in his mind the details of having the parachute repacked, of what he would say to the directors, of making his reports, of seeing that the burnt-out débris was collected and carted back to the works as soon as it cooled, of going up again immediately to restore his shaken nerve, looked up smiling.

"Yes," he said, "I'm all right, it's just my leg. If you'd be so good as to help me across to the aerodrome?"

"Why, of course. Put your arm on my shoulder."

The test-pilot thanked him and smiled again, this time at the other's eagerness, thinking how this was an adventure for him, the making of a tale that he would often "remember with advantages", a story that would bring him silence among his fellow clerks as he related how he had been, for a few glorious moments, a man in a world of men.

# Remembered on Waking

# Remembered on Waking

It was autumn before the letter came. Through all the summer he had waited, oft-times with impatience, spending the long days swimming in the estuary, fishing for bass beyond the bar, wandering over the sands that were flecked with bathers and black cattle or over the deserted hills about Cader Idris, disturbing rabbits and agile mountain sheep, hearing no sound but the rustle of wild streams, the thin twitter of larks, the eerie mew of buzzards and the soft insistent crying of the wind in the short wiry grass. At first the days were long, the evenings after the pubs closed when he browsed among his books, played chess with his father, or walked some giggling girl through twilit lanes, interminable. He missed the rhythm of Service life, the company of those living, as he lived, for flying and flying alone.

But as the visitors drifted away and Welsh was once more heard about the streets, as the cafés closed, the bathing machines were hauled to the shelter of the sand-dunes and the small boats taken to a cove up-river where they would winter, pulling quietly at their seaweed-green ropes, he began to love the idle life, paying less attention day by day to the postman's visits, finding a strange security in the uncertain monotony of his existence.

When the fishermen began to scrape mussels from the river-bed with long-handled rakes he would often go out with them, spending hazy hours on the cold water, hearing only the rubble of the tide against the boats' sides, the splashing of the rakes, the lilting tones of Welsh; watching the many shades of grey. There was the grey of the mist on the fern-golden hills, binding them into purple walls that rose tier upon tier into the rain-laden sky. The grey of the ebbing river, the grey of the wet sandbanks where cormorants stood with wings stretched to dry, the grey of the tumbled village built haphazard up the hillside, still but for the grey strands of smoke floating tentatively upwards, the specks of children playing in the school yard. There was the grey of the oak pier, now deserted and clustered with seaweed and barnacles. There was the everlasting grey of the rain that came with the turning tide, drifting in, soft, warm, intimate, from the Atlantic, sparkling on his shabby tweeds.

And as the rising tide caused them to pull up anchor and row for the mussel tanks by the life-boat slip where the salmon-nets hung listless on their frames, the fishermen would often talk of the "great days" before the war when the slate trade was booming and the morning would find half a dozen sailing vessels waiting in the estuary for the wind to veer to east so that they might wing their ways to the far corners of the earth. Then it was that they grew eloquent, pausing in their quick, easy strokes to tell how wooden ships were once built on the south side of the river, of how there was a railway buried under the dunes, and drawing their rubber boots beneath their seats they would turn to point where cattle-pens and a timber yard once stood.

On other days, sad west winds would blow the clouds on to the hills, the sky would be vivid blue against the sandbanks' yellow and the dunes on the opposite shore glow a dim gold in the elongated rays of the setting sun. Then he would follow the porpoise as they rolled lazily in hunting the placid river or watch the gulls who fought screaming for scraps of refuse and dropped mussels from twenty feet to break on the shore.

He carried the letter about for two days, his fingers often touching its crisp envelope, its phrases bracing his mind, before telling his father. Now that things were decided he felt a sudden disgust at his idleness, an intense desire to work again that was shadowed by the thought of the old man's resultant loneliness. They were playing chess after supper, the sibilant lamplight threading the board with grotesque shadows of the tall chessmen, bringing out the rugged character in the old clergyman's face, enlarging the cosy, book-lined room with heavy gargantuan shadows. They had been silent perhaps an hour, only an occasional "check" punctuating the far-away rumble of the river running over the bar at half-tide, hearing but the persistent hooting of an owl and the intermittent shuddering of the fire as it moved down in the grate, when Robert said in tones too casual to carry conviction: "By the way, I've got a job, Father."

He made no answer till he had moved a bishop, dragging the carved piece so that its ivory rim left a ragged path on the leather surface of the board.

"A flying job?"

He nodded, going on to explain that it was an instructor's post at a flying club in the South of England.

"I'd rather hoped you'd have tired of flying and taken something—something nearer home."

"I'm afraid I'll never tire of flying. Besides, there are no jobs going about here, and anyhow, when they learn that one's been in the Service, employers don't fall on one's neck," he replied, thinking suddenly how his father had aged since his retirement.

"Where is this club?"

"At a place called Best. It's a long way, but I hope to get home sometimes and, of course, there'll be holidays."

"A fortnight is a short time when taken from a year."

"I know. I'm sorry I have to leave you."

"That's all right, my boy. You have to work and you must do what you like. After all, it's your life. Only be careful." He smiled, tapping his queen with a delicate finger. "I seem to have told you that a good many times in the last six years."

"I'll be careful," said Robert. Was that all, he thought, did life bring no more than weariness of body as well as of spirit, no more than to sit patiently and wait for the last great experience of death? Was that all one had to look forward to, no consummation of ambition until things sought had lost their savour, no lasting strength to enjoy the pension so laboriously earned? Did one learn so little but patience, struggle towards tolerance only to become indifferent, did age teach naught but caution? Did one live through so much only to fear the future the more; was to be old, not to be wise, not to be hopeful, only to be careful? Did one live but to weary of life and become the more fearful of death?

Soon he would go through the village to the station, nodding to the retired dons, soldiers, doctors and idle gentry who played with their hunting, fishing, gardening, bridge and pseudo-literary societies; shaking hands with fishermen and villagers, looking for the last time at the string of boats in the river, head to tide, the half-submerged sandbanks, thinking the while of his father in tobacco-dusty clothes, sitting in his corner, looking forward to a few years of emptiness, proud of the son who had left him to loneliness. And as he would take his ticket and when the train would ripple into motion, the river town swing from sight, the telegraph wires rock up and down before the windows, memory would net his mind.

He would remember how his world was once bounded by the high walls of the garden, by the half-understood phrases of his father and the housekeeper, by the hills of the mining valley in which they lived, hills that were then so high, so mystical that his imagination travailled in their vastness. He would remember how first he realized his own individuality, knew in one breath-taking flash of thought (germinated in some undefinable matrix of his subconsciousness) that he was himself, understood that to find peace of mind he would have to struggle with the world, to find stillness of spirit he would have to battle within himself.

He would remember how when sick he lay awake, the firelight throwing a network shadow of the fireguard on to the nursery ceiling, the trains rattling by carrying coal to the Bristol Channel ports, while he thought of time, awed by the words of the Lord's Prayer, "For ever and ever", thinking of eternity till his brain reeled, overwrought by the immensity of something he could only dimly comprehend. How all the lovely sadness of life seemed to be drawn into the autumn when the fern on the hillsides was golden against the October sky, when the hills themselves were a hanging wall of mist, when the air (tart with coming winter) was tinged with garden fires, when the pools in the bog over the railway were gleaming as cold lifeless eyes in the ivory moonlight.

He would remember school, the days all alike as grey beads strung upon the thread of the term. How every evening as he undressed he thought . . . I shall think of this to-morrow, remember how I undressed, folded my clothes into my basket, said my prayers and waited fearfully in my bed after the house tutor had put out the gas (with his usual jokes) wondering if the others were going to beat me. I shall think of this to-morrow and another day will have passed. . . . How this habit became the one reality of the day, a symbol of passing time that comforted him, its regularity introducing a sense of rhythm into the monotonous tenor of his life. He would remember how the blessed thought of the holidays increased through counted days, only to dissolve into the ennui of all but the first week at home.

How he grew older, fell shyly in love with girls

in shops and trains, girls he never dared approach and seldom saw again; how he discovered Dostoievsky and would read into the nights while moths, furry and crassly determined, would circle his candle till they fell burning; how he read through the nights till the chestnut-trees at the bottom of the garden hung as lace against the dawning sky.

He would remember the transitory, timeless dreams of pure beauty that flashed into his mind and were to him as a glimpse of the ground to a pilot flying blind, reassuring him of his position, restoring his confidence in his navigation, lulling uneasiness so that he goes on into the damp coldness, flying happily by instruments and dead reckoning. He would remember his life in the Service. How proud he had been of his first uniform and of being saluted, he would remember the bleakness of Royal Air Force stations, the exhilaration of learning to fly, the beauty of flight itself, the happy comradeship. He would remember . . .

"It's your move, my boy," said his father gently. "Have you been dreaming?"

# Night Exercise

# Night Exercise

It was getting dark as he left the Mess, the western sky stained with a perfect sunset and a light easterly wind blowing coldly off the aerodrome, so that he turned up his great-coat collar and clapped his gloved hands together, thinking with faint longing of the warm ante-room and the circle of chairs about the large brick fireplace.

The sentry outside the guard-room slapped his rifle-butt smartly. Automatically he returned the salute, then gazed upwards, wondering if the wind would remain constant and the weather hold throughout the night. It was peaceful as he walked through the windswept camp, and heard the thin tinkle of radio sets in the barrack blocks cutting through the clatter of a slowly running motor on the tarmac. The hangars, silhouetted big and gaunt against the bleak aerodrome and coloured sky, poured solid light through huge open doors so that the mighty night-bombers, crawling with maintenance crews, threw long straggling shadows on to the concrete aprons.

His own machine was being towed out by a tractor, the tractor-driver swinging his head over each shoulder in turn, watching the mechanics who walked, one beneath each wing, with arms extended to show that the tips were clear of obstructions. He walked quickly through the hangar, his hollow footsteps flung back by the tall roof; ducked beneath the bellies of aircraft on inspections and overhaul; then, with a mechanical salute entered the Flight Commander's office.

A junior officer sat by the telephone engrossed in a thriller. He was young, with smooth, characterless features, absurdly handsome with forage-cap set well over one ear. At his side was a sextant, a pile of maps, logs, parallel rulers and navigational instruments. He looked up as the other entered.

"Hullo, Jimmy!"

"Hullo, old boy."

"I've worked out all the tracks, distances and times. Here's the weather—seems all right."

He nodded as he took the flimsy sheet, then crossed the room to a large map of the British Isles and began to study it, his forehead creased over one eyebrow. At the side of the map were little flags, each marked with a letter and the number of an aircraft. Absently he pulled out one marked "X" and stuck it in at the home aerodrome. Then he walked back to the table and picked up the telephone.

"Langdon here." The voice of his Squadron Leader was crisp and imperious with twenty years of command.

"Brown here, sir. Due off on the first show at eighteen-thirty. Have you seen the weather?"

"Yes—seems good. Got all your instructions?"

"Yes, sir."

"Right. Off you go."

He hung up the receiver and turned to his companion.

"We're off. Get your gubbins aboard."

He went up to the locker-room and began to dress. Sheepskin-lined knee-boots, flying-suit, two pairs of silk gloves, helmet with earphones and microphone attached, sharp pencils and a couple of small flashlamps from his overcoat completed his preparations, together with the parachute he slung over his shoulder.

Crossing to the open window, he peered out at the waiting monoplanes. Grim they seemed, he thought, their broad wings like arms crucified against the dying day. Precise machines, designed, built and flown to one end, to bring destruction to every part of the inhabited globe. Pray God, he'd never have to fly one, with tons of death in its belly, over some darkened town while old men and women and children grovelled in trench and cellar far below.

"Smithers!" his voice went ringing over the tarmac.

"Sir!" came the far-away reply from somewhere in the twilight.

"Spin 'em up!"

"Very good, sir."

As he walked towards the door he could hear his fitter's instructions, followed by "Contact starboard", and the thousand horse-power motor stuttered into life, rocking and twisting on its bearers till the cylinders fired evenly. Then it was joined by its fellow, the fitter throttling down till they ran over quietly, little tongues of flame flickering out of the exhausts.

Even now the slipstream was sufficient to blow his sidcot hard on to his limbs as he walked round the tail, and to send his scarf streaming out beneath his chin. A waiting mechanic wrenched open the door and pulled down the ladder. He climbed inside, buckled on his parachute and then went forward, stooping beneath the cross members and worming his way in the darkness past navigator's table and tall wireless apparatus, where an operator tapped out morse, watching a jittering needle.

The fitter slipped out of the pilot's seat and held the wheel central as the Captain slid in. He settled himself comfortably, adjusted the rudder pedals, pulled up the seat, set the gyro and plugged in his telephones. Then he started to run up the engines, watching a bewildering mass of instruments. As he checked revolutions, temperatures and boost pressures the noise became a solid block of sound that shut out the world, absorbing all sound, blocking his ears. He listened for any irregularity, switching off each circuit of the dual ignition system in turn. His mind was blank, he was part of a machine, working with unthinking efficiency.

Finally satisfied, he nodded to the fitter, who ran nimbly aft and banged the door behind him.

He pulled up his microphone, switching it on.

"Pilot calling navigator!"

"O.K., Skipper, First course one eight two magnetic."

"One eight two magnetic. Thank you. Wireless operator?"

"O.K., sir."

When the front and rear gunners had answered he gave the time, telling the crew to synchronize their watches, then turned off the lights. An answering flicker from below told him that the chocks were away and he let off the brakes and opened the throttles. Ten tons of aeroplane began to move slowly out into the darkness.

Out on the aerodrome a flare path, paraffin flares set at regular intervals, stretched out into wind. As he taxied he began to signal with his top identification light, sending out his letter "X".

Instantly it was answered in green from the first flare, where a group of men huddled about a brazier like gipsies about a camp fire. He rounded the bottom of the path, pumped on flap, felt his brake handle and variable pitch levers (to check that the airscrews were in fine), pulled back the override and began to open the throttles.

Slowly the huge machine began to move, the flares sliding by, flashing yellow light through the windscreen that caught his tense features, expressionless with concentration, as he pushed the heavy wheel forward to bring the tail up. She was accelerating now, the last flare rushing towards him. Judging by the feel that she was almost airborne, he eased the wheel towards him. She bumped twice and began to climb into the darkness.

He bent his head backwards and looked up at the stars, glancing quickly at engine revolutions and airspeed, estimating by these means that the machine was climbing straight and level. As he climbed he pumped off flap, throttled down, slapped the airscrews into coarse; then, turning on a dash light, caught the navigator's eye, putting up his thumb and making a circular movement with his hand. The other repeated the signal to the wireless operator, who nodded and let out a hundred and fifty feet of trailing aerial.

At two thousand feet he began to turn on to his first course. It was exactly half-past six as he crossed the aerodrome and he held up his thumb to the navigator, who set a stop-watch and departed aft to his maps and instruments.

Now, as they left the little cluster of lights that meant the aerodrome and its attendant village, and set off, climbing into the night, the stars, distinct above, seemed more real than the hazy mounds of reflected light that represented distant towns, and the cabin, cramped with the complicated paraphernalia of modern war, became a cosy little room, a tiny world in the dark emptiness of the sky.

Soon they passed over a seaport. He knew it well. By day it sprawled in untidy squalor, its extensive smoke-slurred slums scummed by docks. There seemed no pattern, no attempt at planning; it appeared, as indeed it was, a festering sore on the face of the countryside. But as they slid over it in the darkness, the chains of street lights linked up evenly below, with arteries of brighter blue and green bisecting a beautiful pattern. It was huge and clear-cut and still, the lights ending abruptly at the docks, gleaming on the black hard surface of the water.

The steady roar of the motors became a background of noise of which he was only subconsciously aware. Every few seconds his eye swept his instruments, seeing that each flickering, luminous needle was in its place, while his feet held the bomber steady on her course.

Sometimes a little group of lights that was a village or little town came back out of the darkness to slide beneath a wing, as drifting seaweed seen from the deck of a steamer. The shop lights would fall harshly into the streets, framed in tiny oblong shadows like a strip of film.

An hour and a half later they were fifteen thousand feet above the English Channel. Far below the English coast stretched before them, its line marked by blobs of lights that were coastal towns, lights that reached eastward like a chain of buoys. Somewhere below, too, the Navy were busy and searchlight beams swung in jerky arcs beneath. The Captain turned on to a new course, then signalled to the navigator to take over the controls. When he saw the junior settled on his course, Brown went aft. He bent over the wireless operator's shoulder and read his log, a large book neatly filled with times and hieroglyphics and groups of letters. Then he tapped the Corporal on the shoulder so that the latter looked up quickly, his fingers leaving the key and pulling back his helmet from his ear.

"Take five minutes off . . . got any tea?"

"No, sir."

"Help yourself to mine."

"Thank you, sir."

He walked down the fuselage, feeling his way in the darkness. Amidships, the front gunner, who was also a fitter, stood by the petrol gauges, filling in a large chart pinned on a board. The Captain took it from him and studied the figures, then nodded and handed it back. Now he went into the tail, treading the narrow catwalk gingerly, stooping lower and lower, conscious of a feeling of claustrophobia as he approached the little cabin behind the rudder and elevators. The rear gunner was working on a reconnaissance report with a stub of pencil. The Captain read it carefully.

"Have you been asleep?"

"No, sir."

"Well, make a more detailed report from now on . . . there's much more activity than you've reported."

"I've been doing my best, sir."

"I'm afraid your best isn't quite good enough. Try and improve it."

Walking forward again he thought that the

pilot up in the front seemed very far away and remote at the end of a long tunnel, the soft reddish dash lamp picking out the brighter parts of the intricate machinery which lined the aircraft. There was no sound-proofing and the fuselage was filled with noise, while each part of the structure quivered with the energy of two thousand horse-power.

He looked through a tiny porthole at a town to the north, a skeleton of lights picked clean like the bones of a herring. Somewhere in one of those blocks of darkness was his home, and near his home lived a girl named Hazel. Standing with shoulders hunched, weight supported by elbows that leaned on vibrating longeron, he thought of her, building her semblance in his mind. One day he hoped to marry her, but he was due for discharge from the Air Force in twelve months' time. Perhaps he'd be lucky and land a civil flying job. He sighed. It seemed a pity to be forced to leave the Service which he loved so well, but a Short Service Commission was a Short Service Commission and that was all there was to it.

Suddenly he thought it strange that there should be living people in the tangle of lights below, that it should represent a settled orderly world with

Hazel reading or sewing, her feet twisted up on the sofa beside her, her kitten sleeping with its head in her lap.

The navigator's table, lit by a shaded lamp, was covered with maps and a seeming jungle of instruments topped by a log sheet. This was kept in pencil, lines of closely written figures and abbreviations. He picked it up and read it slowly, his mind, familiar with its involved system, absorbing each detail in sequence, seeking for errors, which he failed to find. Standing by the pilot once more he stooped and read the bombing thermometer. It was twenty degrees below zero Centigrade.

The pilot kicked him gently and pointed ahead. Before them rose a tremendous mass of white cloud, hard and real, towering into heaven. It was almost frightening in its cold, still purity, with the lonely mysticism of its deep valleys enhanced by the moonlight that cast long shadows, lending contrast to the tall face that now blocked their way.

He plugged in his telephone lead and switched on his microphone.

"Go through . . . chance to practise a drop of blind flying."

Swiftly the storm approached and suddenly the

aircraft began to pitch and roll, bumping violently as they flew through the rising currents. Then cloud was all about them, wiping away all distance and altitude, deadening the windows, emphasizing the little interior; and the pilot wriggled in his seat, cut off the cold air carburettor supply, leant slightly forward and concentrated on the miniature aircraft belonging to the artificial horizon. It began to snow, flakes drifting in through the cracks of the windows and powdering the instrument panel. Next, ice crept over the windscreen, first a thin film like the covering of a newly-washed doorstep on a winter's morning, then building rapidly, thickening with astonishing quickness on all leading sections of the machine. The Pitot head became a lump of ice, the airspeed needle flickering and then sagging to zero.

The Captain touched his companion's shoulder and jerked his head, taking the controls again as the other slipped out. He pushed the throttles wide open and began to climb. A few minutes later the bomber was droning through clear sky again, high above jagged peaks of cloud, its wings and fuselage heavy with ice, gleaming white in the moonlight. The Captain called up the navigator as he worked at his table.

"I'm going to stay above this stuff . . . you'll have to get the sextant out and shoot the odd star."

"O.K., old boy."

Six and a half hours after taking-off they were approaching the home aerodrome again. All the village lights were extinguished now and they could see only the camp lights and the hangars blaring light through their open doors and the crucifix of the flare path standing out in the haze that had made the base difficult to find.

The Captain circled the station till his eyes became accustomed to flying at a low altitude, then sent out "X" on his identification lights. He saw a tiny patch of light on the ground as the signaller tested his lamp; then a green winked up at them. He sighed thankfully, switched on lights, adjusted mixture controls and throttled down his motors. The navigator came forward, intimated that the aerial had been wound in, and stood at the pilot's side, one arm resting on the window ledge.

Now the silence was strange to them, the steady pounding of the engines still sounding in their ears so that it was some seconds before they heard the familiar gliding sounds, the wind swishing in the open windows, crying in the undercarriage bracing wires, driving the airscrews so that the motors muttered and popped back in rebellion. He turned in to land, trained fingers slipping the airscrews into fine, cutting off the supply of cool air to the oil systems. At a steady eighty miles an hour he skimmed the trees and bumped the machine down at the first flare for a perfect landing.

"That all for me, cock?" asked the navigator as he climbed out on to the tarmac.

"Yes. Don't hog all the sandwiches before I get up."

A few minutes later he left the locker-room, set forage cap over one eye and walked quickly to the Squadron Leader's office. The latter looked up quickly from a little pile of wireless messages as he saluted.

"All right?"

"Yes, sir. Cissie trip."

The older man smiled.

"Your bombing results weren't too good, and you seemed to have a spot of bother finding this place!"

"It's a bit thick, sir."

"Shouldn't have bothered you if you were dead on your track. How's that navigator of yours shaping?"

"He's going to be good, sir."

"That's fine," said the senior officer and lapsed into silence.

"Will that be all, sir?"

"That'll be all, old boy. Good night!"

"Good night, sir."

He saluted and went out into the brilliant lighting of the hangar. There was no-one about. He could hear a mechanic whistling and the rhythmic thud of a refuelling unit. He hurried towards the Mess. He was cold. He was tired. He was twenty-two years old.

# You've Got to be Dumb to be Happy

# You've Got to be Dumb to be Happy

The second winter on that station was harder. It was a bleak part of East Anglia, beet and corn-growing country with only trees to break the incessant gales from the North Sea that tore the brittle leaves from their branches in early September, found every crevice in our smoky huts and billowed the carpet on the ante-room floor in the temporary Mess.

The contractors were still busy. There were piles of bricks and steel window-frames and tiles by the concrete roads, and great pools of half-mixed plaster. Lorries cut smooth-edged wounds into the mud beneath the wet grass and the half-finished buildings were fringed with steel scaffolding that seemed like a three days' growth on a tramp's chin when we looked down from the air. Only the hangars were finished, but they had no heating and we crouched about the oil-stoves when mist deadened the countryside, burning the soles off our expensive shoes.

Half the aerodrome was waterlogged and there was mud everywhere and nothing to do after dinner, if there was no night flying, except play bridge or sit over the fire in one's room. Usually we changed out of dinner-jackets and drove out of the camp, past the half-frozen sentry and the whores who waited for the troops at the corner of the wood, into rural Suffolk, between the dead fields, the grey leafless trees, the pale cottages neatly thatched with Norfolk reed.

It was a relief to leave the camp and see ordinary life again and drink with strangers and watch the children playing about the lighted shops stuffed with Christmas rubbish. For when one flies the landscape has no reality but is only a flat faraway vista, a panorama with elusive landmarks to be recognized or high ground to be avoided. (A village with a thousand years of tradition only a few untidy cottages washed up about a church, a great industrial area but a glowing mound of light in the darkness.)

Some of the officers went down to the coast, to

the empty seaside resorts with deserted promenades and huge faded tattered posters, or inland to the market towns where the old-fashioned shops had steps and small-paned windows. There they looked for women, driving many times through the streets, scanning the walkers till they saw a likely couple, then, running the car into the gutter, the driver would touch the horn lightly, till the girls came sliding towards them, their smiles and clothes masked by the dusk, stinking of cheap scent, not unattractive so long as they remained silent.

Every other week we flew at nights. Sometimes it was fine and we were high above the sleeping world with the stars real above and the rhythm of the motors sweet in one's ears and the little clusters of lights that were towns floating back till they disappeared beneath one's wing like drifting seaweed. But sometimes the weather was bad and the rain would beat into the open cockpit and we would fly in cloud for hours, the huge night-bombers rocking in the bumps and ice forming on leading edges and on the interplane struts and on the airscrews and we would be lost and frightened in the storm-filled night.

The camp grew, but not in our eyes. Several

officers were posted. Johnson finished his time and went into Dominion Airways. A new pilot was burned to death following a night-flying crash. The Mess Committee put a penny on beer and Wally was placed under close arrest for bouncing another cheque. The police raided Dawn's flat where we used to go after they closed, alleging it was being used for immoral purposes.

The Spring was sad with rain; but occasionally the weather lifted and the shy sunshine fell in moving patches on the country that stretched out to Cambridgeshire, pale and green and lovely, with the new crops breaking through the warm earth.

Dick was a good leader. Time after time he had brought the formation faultlessly over the far hedge with twenty feet to spare, so that we landed well down the aerodrome and the wheels had stopped turning before we reached the circle. Later in the morning we took off on engine test, climbing towards the ceiling of grey clouds that here and there showed a lighter pattern where the sun strove to break through. Below, visibility was bad, the familiar landmarks falsified by light mist, the very shape of the landscape camouflaged by the rain that slid in big tears down the surfaces of our goggles and drove in tiny pricks against our faces.

I put George (as we called the automatic pilot) into operation and we sat silently behind the dual wheels that moved now a little one way, now a little the other, now slightly backwards, now slightly forwards, holding the aircraft in a steady climb with uncanny precision. Dick looked down and I followed his glance. A number of Harts moved swiftly beneath us, locked in squadron vic formation. The grey light, gleaming on their wet silver wings, accentuated their effortless progress over the dim land beneath. It was impossible to estimate their height, difficult to judge their speed, hard to imagine that each unit was a separate machine, flown by a man who sat immobile, strapped in his narrow cockpit, his eyes, hard and alive behind his rain-coated goggles, fixed on his inside neighbour. My companion switched on his microphone.

"Cissy work!" He jerked his head sideways.

I nodded and glanced once more at the array of instruments before me, instinctively checking the oil pressures and temperatures of one engine against the other.

Now we were nearing the base of the clouds. As

I looked up, wondering how thick they were, I felt a vague apprehension, a faint distaste for climbing into their cold, rainful interior that was stifled with a shrug of the shoulders. It was as if I feared the very obscurity of them, the sense of losing oneself in an unknown world. It was as a child lying awake, afraid to allow itself to sleep. For sleep it imagines clearly, not as a relief or rest from toil, but as a surrender of the body, a twisting and blinding of the understanding, akin to death.

Suddenly the clouds were about us, shutting out all movement, all distance, blowing damp and cold against our faces. Minutes passed with only the rhythmic roar of the unsupercharged motors in our ears and the airscrews behind us cutting spinning circles of light in the haziness. Dick sat a little forward, the mist condensing on his helmet and eyebrows and fair moustache.

When we came out there was no sunshine, only a space with another layer of cloud above. It was a lost empty place with no living or moving thing, stretching to a far horizon in every direction, lit by an unseen sun. I took over the controls and flew with the wheels cutting the misty floor so that even the old-fashioned bomber seemed to be travelling fast. Then my companion nudged me in the ribs and pointed to the time. I held her on her course, crossing a silent white valley, then smashing through the opposite hill of cloud. It seemed that this was where the aeroplane really belonged, where the height and depth were in the scene about one, out of sight of the drabness, glitter-shot, so far below.

Dick nudged me in the ribs again and I closed the throttle and let the machine drop into the clouds, the wind crying in the wires, the big wooden airscrews whistling as they overran the motors. I began to sing a dirty song, moving the wheel from side to side to hold the wings level.

We came out south of the aerodrome, easily distinguishable by the glint of the wet tarmac, the gaunt hangars, the even expanse of greener grass.

I throttled down and turned in to land, finding a certain satisfaction in the purely mechanical actions of controlling the aircraft, in trying to fly well with even rates of turn, steady airspeed, good hold-off in a sure approach, sighing with contentment and pushing up my goggles as she dropped lightly on to the wheels and came to rest a few yards from the circle.

A little later I was standing outside the Flight Commander's office. From inside the hangar came the rattle of a drill, the clatter of tool on metal, the voices of the fitters and riggers as they sang and talked and swore. Outside they were filling the aircraft tanks with the rhythmic chugging of re-fuelling unit pumps. I could hear the flap of the wind stocking above me and the wind moaning and whimpering in the wires of the aircraft on the tarmac. There was the smell of petrol and dope and a flight droned overhead, sliding easily across the cloudy sky.

Dick, who had been up again in another air-craft, came in to land. He glided in, held off, then let her go down smoothly. I thought how easy it seemed and how one forgot the sweat of learning to fly, the fears never realized, the ambitions never achieved. Now the machine taxied towards me with Dick sitting very straight, swinging his head from side to side, keeping the aircraft moving with bursts of either engine, distinct twists of the throttle grip that made an airscrew sing in a halo of light and the engine snarl, then lapse to a mutter again.

As the four wheels of the undercarriage rolled on to the tarmac and the machine turned into the wind, the motors sobbed into silence, the air-screws jerked to rest, I watched him, silhouetted against the grey light above the cut-away edge of the cockpit, his strong familiar features framed by shabby leather helmet, topped by rusty goggles. Sometimes, the sight of some intimate scene, villages sprawling like puppies in the sun, rain-smoothed pavements inlaid with the lights of shops, of pub doorways, strangers lost in work, children in the grim world of their play, seem to hold more than the lingering picture thrown on to the screen of the mind. It is as if they mock the introspective glance, taunt the jaded passer-by with elusive, evasive promise.

So, watching Dick, for a flash it seemed that he symbolized youth; youth glorious in untried confidence, unconquerable in hardly-used courage, in its disinclination to profit by the experience of others. Then it was gone, the magic of it a thing shattered so that his image no longer brought a lump to my throat. It was only my friend, a hard-drinking flying-man who was ragged in Mess for his good looks.

It was a supper night, so after tea I changed into flannels and strolled down the corridor past the open door of Dick's room. He was brushing his hair and grinned at my reflection in the mirror.

"Shocking hair oil, this stuff of yours!"

I went in and sat on his bed. There was hardly room for the tin washbasin, chest of drawers, wardrobe, table and bookcase, while an iron stove pipe ran through the ceiling. The window gave an interrupted view of the next hut a few yards away and an oblong strip of sky. On the wall over the bed were several drawings of naked women, a large photograph of a very pretty girl and a placard from a dance-hall proclaiming that "No Dressing or Undressing was allowed in these Lavatories".

"Don't tell my mother I'm in the Air Force," screamed another notice; "she still thinks I'm playing a piano in a brothel." The bookshelves contained several German beer mugs and some Service publications with the uninserted amendments neatly stacked at the side. In common with other rooms in the hut, a wireless played at full volume. One had to shout to make oneself heard.

"What are we doing to-night?" Dick said.

"Oh, I don't know, we might go down to the *Bear* for a quiet drink."

"Euh! euh! not me, I'm economizing."

"So that's why you sent your batman round to borrow my soap?"

"Surely. I've got to economize this month. My Mess bill's fifteen quid already," he laughed. "I don't know how I'm going to find the cash, especially as my tailors get a fiver on a banker's order."

"You'll manage," I said.

One of the sister squadron's aircraft flew over on a night flying test, a sudden roar of sound, a shadow flickering across the window.

"We might go to the movies," Dick said.

It was getting dark when we arrived at the *Bear*. The cobbled yard was full of cars and through the open windows of the bar I could see that there were many of my brother officers inside, and women too, brave with make-up, their charming inane chatter glittering in the pattern of sound. In the bar we were immediately surrounded, drinks were pushed into our hands. Dick's, as usual, was neat Scotch.

Someone told the story of the bomber captain who handed over to his second pilot at twenty-five feet. The second pilot's name was Newton. I went over to a man who sat in the corner. He had recently been discharged from hospital after a crash.

"I thought you were on sick leave?"

"I am."

"But you live . . . ?"

"In Scotland. I went home for a month. But after a few days, well . . . "

"You don't fit any more."

But most of the talk was of shop, of the recent exercises, happenings on various stations and when we were to get the new monoplanes. It was all so easy now with the bright lights gleaming on tankard and bottle and a pretty girl at one's side. One was a night-bomber pilot, courageous and confident, there was nothing in the game, it was pansy.

Only occasionally, as the door opened to admit someone with the rain sliding from the edge of his hat, shaking himself like an indignant dog, one was reminded of the darkness outside which waited for us, patient and quiet, because there was no need for haste.